D1074789

AUG   2005

INSIDE JOB

INSIDE JOB

BY

CONNIE WILLIS

SUBTERRANEAN PRESS ✠ 2005

Subterranean Press

PO Box 190106

Burton, MI 48519

subpress@earthlink.net

1

*"Nobody ever went broke underestimating
the intelligence of the American people."*

— H.L. MENCKEN —

◆ ◆ ◆

"It's me, Rob," Kildy said when I picked up the phone. "I want you to go with me to see somebody Saturday."

Usually when Kildy calls, she's bubbling over with details. "You've *got* to see this psychic cosmetic surgeon, Rob," she'd crowed the last time. "His specialty is liposuction, and you can *see* the tube coming out of his sleeve. And that's not all. The fat he's supposed to be suctioning out of their thighs is that goop they use in McDonald's milkshakes. You can smell the vanilla! It wouldn't fool a five-year-old, so of course half the women in Hollywood are buying it hook, line, and sinker. We've *got* to do a story on him, Rob!"

I usually had to say, "Kildy—Kildy—Kildy!" before I could get her to shut up long enough to tell me where he was performing.

But this time all she said was, "The seminar's at one o'clock at the Beverly Hills Hilton. I'll meet you in the parking lot," and hung up before I could ask her if the somebody she wanted me to see was a pet channeler or a vedic-force therapist, and how much it was going to cost.

I called her back.

"The tickets are on me," she said.

7

If Kildy had her way, the tickets would always be on her, and she can more than afford it. Her father's a director at Dreamworks, her current stepmother heads her own production company, and her mother's a two-time Oscar winner. And Kildy's rich in her own right—she only acted in four films before she quit the business for a career in debunking, but one of them was the surprise top grosser of the year, and she'd opted for shares instead of a salary.

But she's ostensibly my employee, even though I can't afford to pay her enough to keep her in toenail polish. The least I can do is spring for expenses, and a barely-known channeler shouldn't be too bad. Medium Charles Fred, the current darling of the Hollywood set, was only charging two hundred a seance.

"*The Jaundiced Eye* is paying for the tickets," I said firmly. "How much?"

"Seven hundred and fifty apiece for the group seminar," she said. "Fifteen hundred for a private enlightenment audience."

"The tickets are on you," I said.

"Great,"she said. "Bring the Sony vidcam."

"Not the little one?" I asked. Most psychic events don't allow recording devices—they make it too easy to spot the earpieces and wires—and the Hasaka is small enough to be smuggled in.

"No," she said, "bring the Sony. See you Saturday, Rob. Bye."

"Wait," I said. "You haven't told me what this guy does."

"Woman. She's a channeler. She channels an entity named Isis," Kildy said and hung up again.

I was surprised. We don't usually waste our time on channelers. They're no longer trendy. Right now mediums like Charles Fred and Yogi Magaputra and assorted sensory therapists (aroma-, sonic-, auratic-) are the rage.

It's also an exercise in frustration, since there's no way to prove whether someone's channeling or not, unless they claim to be channeling Abraham Lincoln (like Randall Mars) or Nefertiti (like Hanh Nah.) In that case you can challenge their facts— Nefertiti could *not* have had an affair with Alexander the Great, who wasn't born till a thousand years later, and she was *not* Cleopatra's cousin—but most of them channel hundred thousand-year-old sages or high priests of Lemuria, and there are no physical manifestations.

They've learned their lesson from the Victorian spiritualists (who kept getting caught), so there's no ectoplasm or ghostly trumpets or double-exposed photographic plates. Just a deep, hollow voice that sounds like a cross between Obi Wan Kenobi and Basil Rathbone. Why is it that channeled "entities" all have British accents? And speak King James Bible English?

And why was Kildy willing to waste fifteen hundred bucks— correction, twenty-two fifty; she'd already been to the seminar once—to have me see this Isis? The channeler must have a new gimmick. I'd noticed a couple of people advertising themselves as "angel channelers" in the local psychic rag, but Isis wasn't an angel name. Egyptian channeler? Goddess conduit?

I looked "Isis-channeler" up on the net. At first I couldn't find any references, even using Google. I tried skeptics.org and finally Marty Rumboldt, who runs a website that tracks psychics.

"You're spelling it wrong, Rob," he e-mailed me back. "It's Isus."

Which should have occurred to me. The channelers of Lazaris, Kochise, and Merlynn all use variations on historical names (probably from some fear of spiritual slander lawsuits), and more than one channeler's prone to "inventive" spelling: Joye Wildde. And Emmanual.

I googled "Isus." He—bad sign, the channeler didn't even know Isis was female—was the "spirit entity" channeled by somebody named Ariaura Keller. She'd started in Salem, Massachusetts (a breeding ground for psychics), moved to Sedona (another one), and then headed west and worked her way down the coast, appearing in Seattle, the other Salem, Eugene, Berkeley, and now Beverly Hills. She had six afternoon seminars and two week-long "spiritual immersions" scheduled for L.A., along with private "individually scheduled enlightenment audiences" with Isus. She'd written two books, *The Voice of Isus* and *On the Receiving End* (with links to amazon.com) and you could read her bio: "I knew from childhood that I was destined to be a channel for the Truth," and extracts from her speeches: "The earth is destined to witness a transforming spiritual event," on-line. She sounded just like every other channeler I'd ever heard.

And I'd sat through a bunch of them. Back at the height of their popularity (and before I knew better), *The Jaundiced Eye* had done a six-part series on them, starting with M.Z. Lord and running on through Joye Wildde, Todd Phoenix, and Taryn Kryme, whose "entity" was a giggly six-year-old kid from Atlantis. It was the longest six months of my life. And it didn't have any impact at all on the business. It was tax evasion and mail fraud charges that had put an end to the fad, not my hardhitting exposés.

Ariaura Keller didn't have a criminal record (at least under that name), and there weren't many articles about her. And no mention of any gimmick. "The electric, amazing Isus shares his spiritual wisdom and helps you find your own inner-centeredness and soul-unenfoldment." Nothing new there.

Well, whatever it was that had gotten Kildy interested in her, I'd find out on Saturday. In the meantime, I had an article on Charles Fred to write for the December issue, a book on intelligent design (the latest ploy for getting creationism into the schools and evolution out) to review, and a past-life chiropractor to go see. He claimed his patients' backaches came from hauling blocks of stone to Stonehenge and/or the Pyramids. (The Pyramids had in fact been a big job, but over the course of three years in business he'd told over two thousand patients they'd gotten their herniated discs at Stonehenge, every single one of them while setting the altar stone in place.)

And he was actually credible compared to Charles Fred, who was having amazing success communicating highly specific messages from the dead to their grieving relatives. I was convinced he was doing something besides the usual cold reading and shills to get the millions he was raking in, but so far I hadn't been able to figure out what, and every lead I managed to come up with went nowhere.

I didn't think about the "electric, amazing Isus" again till I was driving over to the Hilton Saturday. Then it occurred to me that I hadn't heard from Kildy since her phone call. Usually she drops by the office every day, and if we're going somewhere calls three or four times to reconfirm where and when we're meeting. I wondered if the seminar was still on, or if she'd forgotten all about it. Or suddenly gotten tired of being a debunker and gone back to being a movie star.

I'd been waiting for that to happen ever since the day just over eight months ago when, just like the gorgeous dame in a Bogie movie, she'd walked into my office and asked if she could have a job.

There are three cardinal rules in the skeptic business. The first one is, "Extraordinary claims require extraordinary evidence," and the second one is, "If it seems too good to be true, it probably is." And if anything was ever too good to be true, it's Kildy. She's not only rich and movie-star beautiful, but intelligent, and, unlike everyone else in Hollywood, a complete skeptic, even though, as she told me that first day, Shirley MacLaine had dandled her on her knee and her own mother would believe anything, "no matter how ridiculous, which is probably why her marriage to my father lasted nearly six years."

She was now on Stepmother Number Four, who had gotten her the role in the surprise top grosser, "which made almost as much money as *Lord of the Rings* and enabled me to take early retirement."

"Retirement?" I'd said. "Why would you want to retire? You could have—"

"Starred in *The Hulk III,*" she said, "and been on the cover of the *Globe* with Ben Affleck. Or with my lawyer in front of a rehab center. I know, it was tough to give all that up."

She had a point, but that didn't explain why she'd want to go to work for a barely-making-it magazine like *The Jaundiced Eye.* Or why she'd want to go to work at all.

I said so.

"I've already tried the whole 'fill your day with massages and lunch at Ardani's and sex with your trainer' scene, Rob," she said. "It was even worse than *The Hulk.* Plus, the lights and makeup *destroy* your complexion."

I found that hard to believe. She had skin like honey.

"And then my mother took me to this luminescence reading—she's into all those things, psychics and past-life regression and intuitive healing, and the guy doing the reading—"

"Lucius Windfire," I'd said. I'd been working on an expose of him for the last two months.

"Yes, Lucius Windfire," she'd said. "He claimed he could read your mind by determining your vedic fault lines, which consisted of setting candles all around you and 'reading' the wavering of the flames. It was obvious he was a fake—you could see the earpiece he was getting his information over—but everybody there was eating it up, especially my mother. He'd already talked her into private sessions that set her back ten thousand dollars. And I thought, somebody should put him out of business, and then I thought, that's what I want to do with my life, and I looked up 'debunkers' on-line and found your magazine, and here I am."

I'd said, "I can't possibly pay you the kind of money you're—"

"Your going rate for articles is fine," she'd said and flashed me her better-than-Julia-Roberts smile. "I just want the chance to do something useful and sensible with my life."

And for the last eight months she'd been working with me on the magazine. She was wonderful—she knew everybody in Hollywood, which meant she could get us into invitation-only stuff, and heard about new spiritual fads even before I did. She was also willing to do anything, from letting herself be hypnotized to stealing chicken guts from psychic surgeons to proofreading galleys. And fun to talk to, and gorgeous, and much too good for a small-time skeptic, like me.

And I knew it was just a matter of time before she got bored with debunking and went back to going to premieres and driving around in her Jaguar, but she didn't. "Have you ever *worked* with Ben Affleck?" she'd said when I told her she was too beautiful not to still be in the movies. "You couldn't *pay* me to go back to that."

She wasn't in the parking lot, and neither was her Jaguar, and I wondered, as I did every day, if this was the day she'd decided to call it quits. No, there she was, getting out of a taxi. She was wearing a honey-colored pantsuit the same shade as her hair and designer sunglasses, and she looked, as always, too good to be true. She saw me and waved, and then reached back in for two big throw pillows.

Shit. That meant we were going to have to sit on the floor again. These people made a fortune scamming people out of their not-so-hard-earned cash. You'd think they could afford chairs.

I walked over to her. "I take it we're going in together," I said, since the pillows were a matching pair, purple brocade jobs with tassels at the corners.

"Yes," Kildy said. "Did you bring the Sony?"

"Yeah," I said. "I still think I should have brought the Hasaka."

She shook her head. "They're doing body checks. I don't want to give them an excuse to throw us out. When they fill out the nametags, give them your real name."

"We're not using a cover?" I asked. Psychics often use skeptics in the audience as an excuse for failure: the negative vibrations made it impossible to contact the spirits, etc. A couple of them had even banned me from their performances, claiming I disturbed the cosmos with my nonbelieving presence. "Do you think that's a good idea?"

"We don't have any choice," she said. "When I came last week, I was with my publicist, so I had to use my own name, and I didn't think it mattered—we never do channelers. Besides, the ushers recognized me. So our cover is, I was so impressed with Ariaura that I talked you into coming to see her."

"Which is pretty much the truth," I said. "What exactly is her gimmick, that you thought I should see her?"

"I don't want to prejudice you beforehand." She glanced at her Vera Wang watch and handed me one of the pillows. "Let's go."

We went into the lobby and over to a table under a lilac-and-silver banner proclaiming "Presenting Ariaura and the Wisdom of Isus" and under it, "Believe and It Will Happen." Kildy told the woman at the table our names.

"Oh, I loved you in that movie, Miss Ross," she said and handed us lilac-and-silver nametags and motioned us toward another table next to the door, where a Russell Crowe type in a lilac polo shirt was doing security checks.

14

"Any cameras, tape recorders, videocams?" he asked us.

Kildy opened her bag and took out an Olympus. "Can't I take *one* picture?" she pleaded. "I won't use the flash or anything. I just wanted to get a photo of Ariaura."

He plucked the Olympus neatly from her fingers. "Autographed 8x10 glossies can be purchased in the waiting area."

"Oh, *good*," she said. She really should have stayed in acting.

I relinquished the videocam. "What about videos of today's performance?" I said after he finished frisking me.

He stiffened. "Ariaura's communications with Isus are not performances. They are unique glimpses into a higher plane. You can order videos of today's experience in the waiting area," he said, pointing toward a pair of double doors.

The "waiting area" was a long hall lined with tables full of books, videos, audiotapes, chakra charts, crystal balls, aromatherapy oils, amulets, Zuni fetishes, wisdom mobiles, healing stones, singing crystal bowls, amaryllis roots, aura cleansers, pyramids, and assorted other New Age junk, all with the lilac-and-silver Isus logo.

The third cardinal rule of debunking, and maybe the most important, is "Ask yourself, what do they get out of it?" or, as the Bible (source of many scams) puts it, "By their fruits shall ye know them."

And if the prices on this stuff were any indication, Ariaura was getting a hell of a lot out of it. The 8x10 glossies were $28.99, $35.00 with Ariaura's signature. "And if you want it signed by Isus," the blonde guy behind the table said, "it's a hundred. He's not always willing to sign."

I could see why. His signature (done in Magic Marker) was a string of complicated symbols that looked like a cross between Elvish runes and Egyptian hieroglyphics whereas Ariaura's was a script "A" followed by a formless scrawl.

Videotapes of her previous seminars—Volumes 1-20—cost a cool sixty apiece, and Ariaura's "sacred amulet" (which looked like something you'd buy on the Home Shopping Network) cost nine hundred and fifty (box extra). People were snapping them up like hotcakes, along with Celtic pentacles, meditation necklaces, dreamcatcher earrings, worry beads, and toe rings with your zodiac sign on them.

Kildy bought one of the outrageously priced stills (no signature) and three of the videos, cooing, "I just *loved* her last seminar," gave the guy selling them her autograph, and we went into the auditorium.

It was hung with rose, lilac, and silver chiffon floorlength banners and a state-of-the-art lighting system. Stars and planets rotated overhead, and comets occasionally whizzed by. The stage end of the auditorium was hung with gold mylar, and in the center of the stage was a black pyramid-backed throne. Apparently Ariaura did not intend to sit on the floor like the rest of us.

At the door, ushers clad in mostly unbuttoned lilac silk shirts and tight pants took our tickets. They all looked like Tom Cruise, which would be par for the course even if this wasn't Hollywood.

Sex has been a mainstay of the psychic business since Victorian days. Half the appeal of early table-rapping had been the filmy-draperies-and-nothing-else-clad female "spirits" who drifted tantalizingly among the male séance goers, fogging up their spectacles and preventing them from thinking clearly. Sir William Crookes, the famous British chemist, had been so besotted by an obviously fake medium's sexy daughter that he'd staked his scientific reputation on the medium's dubious authenticity, and nowadays it's no accident that most channelers are male and given to chest-baring Rudolph-Valentino-like robes. Or, if they're female, have buff, handsome ushers to distract the women in the audience. If you're drooling over them, you're not likely to spot the wires and chicken guts or realize what they're saying is nonsense.. It's the oldest trick in the book.

One of the ushers gave Kildy a Tom Cruise smile and led her to the end of a cross-legged row on the very hard-looking floor. I was glad Kildy had brought the pillows.

I plopped mine down next to hers and sat down on it. "This had better be good," I said.

"Oh, it will be," a fifty-ish redhead wearing the sacred amulet and a diamond as big as my fist said. "I've seen Ariaura, and she's wonderful." She reached into one of the three lilac shopping bags she'd stuck between us and pulled out a needlepoint lavender pillow that said, "Believe and It Will Happen."

I wondered if that applied to her believing her pillow was large enough to sit on, because it was about the same size as the rock on her finger, but as soon as they'd finished organizing the rows, the ushers came around bearing stacks of plastic-covered cushions (the kind rented at football games, only lilac) for ten bucks apiece.

The woman next to me took three, and I counted ten other people in our row, and eleven in the row ahead of us shelling out for them. Eighty rows times ten, to be conservative. A cool eight thousand bucks, just to sit down, and who knows how much profit in all those lilac shopping bags. "By their fruits shall ye know them."

I looked around. I couldn't see any signs of shills or a wireless setup, but, unlike psychics and mediums, channelers don't need them. They give out general advice, couched in New Age terms.

"Isus is absolutely astonishing," my neighbor confided. "He's so *wise!* Much better than Romtha. He's responsible for my deciding to leave Howard. 'To thine inner self be true,' Isus said, and I realized Howard had been *blocking* my spiritual ascent—"

"Were you at last Saturday's seminar?" Kildy leaned across me to ask.

"*No.* I was in Cancun, and I was just decimated when I realized I'd missed it. I made Tio bring me back early so I could come today. I desperately need Isus's wisdom about the divorce. Howard's claiming Isus had nothing to do with my decision, that I left him because the pre-nup had expired, and he's threatening to call Tio as—"

But Kildy had lost interest and was leaning across *her* to ask a pencil-thin woman in the full lotus position if she'd seen Ariaura before. She hadn't, but the one on her right had.

"Last Saturday?" Kildy asked.

She hadn't. She'd seen her six weeks ago in Eugene.

I leaned towards Kildy and whispered, "What happened last Saturday?"

"I think they're starting, Rob," she said, pointing at the stage, where absolutely nothing was happening, and got off her pillow and onto her knees.

"What are you doing?" I whispered.

She didn't answer that either. She reached inside her pillow, pulled out an orange pillow the same size as the "Believe and It Will Happen" cushion, handed it to me, and arranged herself gracefully on the large tasseled one. As soon as she was cross-legged, she took the orange pillow back from me and laid it across her knees.

"Comfy?" I asked.

"Yes, thank you," she said, turning her movie-star smile on me.

I leaned toward her. "You sure you don't want to tell me what we're doing here?"

"Oh, look, they're starting," she said, and this time they were.

18

A Brad-Pitt lookalike stepped out on stage holding a hand mike and gave us the ground rules. No flash photos (even though they'd confiscated all the cameras). No applause (it breaks Ariaura's concentration). No bathroom breaks. "The cosmic link with Isus is extremely fragile," Brad explained, "and movement or the shutting of a door can break that connection."

Right. Or else Ariaura had learned a few lessons from EST, including the fact that people who are distracted by their bladders are less likely to spot gobbledegook, like the stuff Brad was spouting right now:

"Eighty thousand years ago Isus was a high priest of Atlantis. He lived for three hundred years before he departed this earthly plane and acquired the wisdom of the ages—"

What ages? The Paleolithic and Neolithic? Eighty thousand years ago we were still living in trees.

"—he spoke with the oracle at Delphi, he delved into the Sacred Writings of Rosicrucian—"

Rosicrucian?

"Now watch as Ariaura calls him from the Cosmic All to share his wisdom with you."

The lights deepened to rose, and the chiffon banners began to blow in, as if there was a breeze behind them. Correction, state-of-the-art lighting *and* fans.

The gale intensified, and for a moment, I wondered if Ariaura was going to swoop in on a wire, but then the gold mylar parted, revealing a curving black stairway, and Ariaura, in a purple velvet caftan and her sacred amulet, descended it to the strains of Holst's *Planets* and went to stand dramatically in front of her throne.

The audience paid no attention to the "no applause" edict, and Ariaura seemed to expect it. She stood there for at least two minutes, regally surveying the crowd. Then she raised her arms as if delivering a benediction and lowered them again, quieting the crowd. "Welcome, Seekers after Divine Truth," she said in a peppy, Oprah-type voice, and there was more applause. "We're going to have a wonderful spiritual experience together here today and achieve a new plane of enlightenment."

More applause.

"But you mustn't applaud me. I am only the conduit through which Isus passes, the vessel he fills. Isus first came to me, or, rather, I should say, *through* me, five years ago, but I was afraid. I didn't want to believe it. It took me nearly a whole year to accept that I had become the focus for cosmic energies beyond the reality we know. It's the wisdom of his highly evolved spirit you'll hear today, not mine. If..." a nice theatrical pause here, "...he deigns to come to us. For Isus is a sage, not a servant to be bidden. He comes when he wills. Mayhap he will be among us this afternoon, mayhap not."

In a pig's eye. These women weren't going to shell out seven hundred and fifty bucks for a no-show, even if this was Beverly Hills. I'd bet the house Isus showed up right on cue.

"Isus will come only if our earthly plane is in alignment with the cosmic," Ariaura said, "if the auratic vibrations are right." She looked sternly out at the audience. "If any of you are harboring negative vibrations, contact cannot be made."

Uh-oh, here it comes, I thought, and waited for her to look straight at the two of us and tell us to leave, but she didn't. She merely said, "Are all of you thinking positive thoughts, feeling positive emotions? Are you all believing?"

You bet.

"I sense that every one of you is thinking positive thoughts," Ariaura said."Good. Now, to bring Isus among us, you must help me. You must each calm your center." She closed her eyes. "You must concentrate on your inner soul-self."

I glanced around the audience. Over half of the women had their eyes shut, and many had folded their hands in an attitude of prayer. Some swayed back and forth, and the woman next to me was droning, "Om." Kildy had her eyes closed, her orange pillow clasped to her chest.

"Align...align..." Ariaura chanted, and then with finality, "Align." There was another theatrical pause.

"I will now attempt to contact Isus," she said. "The focusing of the astral energy is a dangerous and difficult operation. I must ask that you remain perfectly quiet and still while I am preparing myself."

The woman next to me obediently stopped chanting, "Om," and everyone opened their eyes. Ariaura closed hers and leaned back in her throne, her ring-covered hands draped over the ends of the arms. The lights went down and the music came up, the theme from Holst's "Mars." Everyone, including Kildy, watched breathlessly.

Ariaura jerked suddenly as if she were being electrocuted and clutched the arms of the throne. Her face contorted, her mouth twisting and her head shaking. The audience gasped. Her body jerked again, slamming back against the throne, and she went into a series of spasms and writhings, with more shaking. This went on for a full minute, while "Mars" built slowly behind her and the spotlight morphed to pink. The music cut off, and she slumped lifelessly back against the throne.

She remained there for a nicely-timed interval, and then sat up stiffly, staring straight ahead, her hands lying loosely on the throne's arms. "I am Isus!" she said in a booming voice that was the dead ringer for "Who dares to approach the great Oz?"

"I am the Enlightened One, a servant unto that which is called the Text and the First Source. I have come from the ninth level of the astral plane," she boomed, "to aid you in your spiritual journeys."

21

So far it was an exact duplicate of Romtha, right down to the pink light and the number of the astral plane level, but next to me Kildy was leaning forward expectantly.

"I have come to speak the truth," Isus boomed, "to reveal to thou thine higher self."

I leaned over to Kildy and whispered, "Why is it they never learn how to use 'thee' and 'thou' correctly on the astral plane?"

"Shh," Kildy hissed, intent on what Isus was saying.

"I bring you the long-lost wisdom of the kingdom of Lemuria and the prophecies of Antinous to aid thee in these troubled days, for thou livest in a time of tribulation. The last days these are of the Present Age, days filled with anxiety and terrorist attacks and dysfunctional relationships. But I say unto ye, thou must not look without but within, for thee alone are responsible for your happiness, and if that means getting out of a bad relationship, make it so. Seek you must your own inner isness and create thou must thine own inner reality. Thee art the universe."

I don't know what I'd been expecting. *Something,* at least, but this was just the usual New Age nonsense, a mush of psychobabble, self-help tips, pseudo-scripture, and Chicken Soup for the Soul.

I sneaked a glance at Kildy. She was still sitting forward, clutching her pillow tightly to her chest, her beautiful face intent, her mouth slightly open. I wondered if she could actually have been taken in by Ariaura. It's always a possibility, even with skeptics. Kildy wouldn't be the first one to be fooled by a cleverly done illusion.

But this wasn't cleverly done. It wasn't even original. The Lemuria stuff was Richard Zephyr, the "Thou art the universe" stuff was Shirley MacLaine, and the syntax was pure Yoda.

And this was Kildy we were talking about. Kildy, who never fell for anything, not even that devic levitator. She had to have a good reason for shelling out over two thousand bucks for this, but so far I was stumped. "What exactly is it you wanted me to see?" I murmured.

"*Shhh.*"

"But fear not," Ariaura said, "for a New Age is coming, an age of peace, of spiritual enlightenment, when thou—doing here listening to this confounded claptrap?"

I looked up sharply. Ariaura's voice had changed in midsentence from Isus's booming bass to a gravelly baritone, and her manner had, too. She leaned forward, hands on her knees, scowling at the audience. "It's a lot of infernal gabble," she said belligerently.

I glanced at Kildy. She had her eyes fixed on the stage.

"This hokum is even worse than the pretentious bombast you hear in the chautauqua," the voice croaked.

Chautauqua? I thought. What the—?

"But there you sit, with your mouths hanging open, like the rubes at an Arkansas camp meeting, listening to a snakecharming preacher, waiting for her to fix up your romances and cure your gallstones—"

The woman next to Kildy glanced questioningly at us and then back at the stage. Two of the ushers standing along the wall exchanged frowning glances, and I could hear whispering from somewhere in the audience.

"Have you yaps actually fallen for this mystical mumbojumbo? Of course you have. This is America, home of the imbecile and the ass!" the voice said, and the whispering became a definite murmur.

"What in the—?" a woman behind us said, and the woman next to me gathered up her bags, stuffed her "Believe" pillow into one of them, stood up, and began to step over people to get to the door.

One of the ushers signalled someone in the control booth, and the lights and Holst's "Venus" began to come up. The emcee took a hesitant step out onto the stage.

"You sit there like a bunch of gaping primates, ready to buy anyth—" Ariaura said, and her voice changed abruptly back to the basso of Isus, "—but the Age of Spiritual Enlightenment cannot begin until each of thou beginnest thy own journey."

The emcee stopped in mid-step, and so did the murmuring. And the woman who'd been next to me and who was almost to the door. She stood there next to it, holding her bags and listening.

"And believe. All of you, casteth out the toxins of doubt and skepticism now. *Believe* and it will happen."

She must be back on script. The emcee gave a sigh of relief, and retreated back into the wings, and the woman who'd been next to me sat down where she'd been standing, bags and pillows and all. The music faded, and the lights went back to rose.

"Believe in thine inner Soul-Self," Ariaura/Isus said. "Believe, and let your spiritual unfoldment begin." She paused, and the ushers looked up nervously. The emcee poked his head out from the gold mylar drapes.

"I grow weary," she said. "I must return now to that higher reality from whence I cameth. Fear not, for though I no longer share this earthly plane with thee, still I am with thou." She raised her arm stiffly in a benediction/Nazi salute, gave a sharp shudder, and then slumped forward in a swoon that would have done credit to Gloria Swanson. Holst's "Venus" began again, and she sat up, blinking, and turned to the emcee, who had come out onstage again.

"Did Isus speak?" she asked him in her original voice.

"Yes, he did," the emcee said, and the audience burst into thunderous applause, during which he helped her to her feet and handed her over to two of the ushers, who walked her, leaning heavily on them, up the black stairway and out of sight.

As soon as she was safely gone, the emcee quieted the applause and said, "Copies of Ariaura's books and videotapes are available outside in the waiting area. If you wish to arrange for a private audience, see me or one of the ushers," and everyone began gathering up their pillows and heading for the door.

"Wasn't he *wonderful?*" a woman ahead of us in the exodus said to her friend. "So authentic!"

"*Is Los Angeles the worst town in America,
or only next to the worst? The skeptic,
asked the original question, will say yes,
the believer will say no. There you have it.*"

— H.L. MENCKEN —

◆ ◆ ◆

Kildy and I didn't talk till we were out of the parking lot and
on Wilshire, at which point Kildy said, "Now do you
understand why I wanted you to see it for yourself, Rob?"

"It was interesting, all right. I take it she did the same thing at
the seminar you went to last week?"

She nodded. "Only last week two people walked out."

"Was it the exact same spiel?"

"No. It didn't last quite as long—I don't know how long
exactly, it caught me by surprise—and she used slightly different
words, but the message was the same. And it happened the same
way—no warning, no contortions, her voice just changed abruptly in mid-sentence. So what do you think's going on, Rob?"

I turned onto LaBrea. "I don't know, but lots of channelers do
more than one 'entity.' Joye Wildde does two, and before Hans
Lightfoot went to jail, he did half a dozen."

Kildy looked skeptical. "Her promotional material doesn't say
anything about multiple entities."

27

"Maybe she's tired of Isus and wants to switch to another spirit. When you're a channeler, you can't just announce, 'Coming soon: Isus II.' You've got to make it look authentic. So she introduces him with a few words one week, a couple of sentences the next, etcetera."

"She's introducing a new and improved spirit who yells at the audience and calls them imbeciles and rubes?" she said incredulously.

"It's probably what channelers call a 'dark spirit,' a so-called bad entity that tries to lead the unwary astray. Todd Phoenix used to have a nasty voice break in in the middle of White Feather's spiel and make heckling comments. It's a useful trick. It reinforces the idea that the psychic's actually channelling, and anything inconsistent or controversial the channeler says can be blamed on the bad spirit."

"But Ariaura didn't even seem to be aware there *was* a bad spirit, if that's what it was supposed to be. Why would it tell the audience to go home and stop giving their money to a snake-oil vendor like Ariaura?"

A snake oil vendor? That sounded vaguely familiar, too. "Is that what she said last week? Snake-oil vendor?"

"Yes," she said. "Why? Do you know who she's channeling?"

"No," I said, frowning, "but I've heard that phrase somewhere. And the line about the chautauqua."

"So it's obviously somebody famous," Kildy said.

But the historical figures channelers did were always instantly recognizable. Randall Mars's Abraham Lincoln began every sentence with "Four score and seven years ago," and the others were all equally obvious. "I wish I'd gotten Ariaura's little outburst on tape," I said.

"We did," Kildy said, reaching over the backseat and grabbing her orange pillow. She unzipped it, reached inside, and brought out a micro-vidcam. "Ta-da! I'm sorry I didn't get last week's. I didn't realize they were frisking people." She fished in the pillow

28

again and brought out a sheet of paper. "I had to run to the bathroom and scribble down what I could remember."

"I thought they didn't let people go to the bathroom."

She grinned at me. "I gave an Oscar-worthy performance of an actress they'd let out of rehab too soon."

I glanced at the list at the next stoplight. There were only a few phrases on it: the one she'd mentioned, and "I've never seen such shameless bilge," and "you'd have to be a pack of deluded half-wits to believe something so preposterous."

"That's all?"

She nodded. "I told you, it didn't last nearly as long last time. And since I wasn't expecting it, I missed most of the first sentence."

"That's why you were asking at the seminar about buying the videotape?"

"Unh-huh, although I doubt if there's anything on it. I've watched her last three videos, and there's no sign of Entity Number Two."

"But it happened at the seminar you went to and at this one. Has it occurred to you it might have happened *because* we were there?" I pulled into a parking space in front of the building where *The Jaundiced Eye* has its office.

"But—" she said.

"The ticket-taker could have alerted her that we were there," I said. I got out and opened her door for her, and we started up to the office. "Or she could have spotted us in the audience—you're not the only one who's famous. My picture's on every psychic wanted poster on the West Coast—and she decided to jazz up the performance a little by adding another entity. To impress us."

"That can't be it."

I opened the door. "Why not?"

"Because it's happened at least twice before," she said, walking in and sitting down in the only good chair. "In Berkeley and Seattle."

"How do you know?"

"My publicist's ex-boyfriend's girlfriend saw her in Berkeley—that's how my publicist found out about Ariaura—so I got her number and called her and asked her, and she said Isus was talking along about tribulation and thee being the universe, and all of a sudden this other voice said, 'What a bunch of boobs!' She said that's how she knew Ariaura was really channeling, because if it was fake she'd hardly have called the audience names."

"Well, there's your answer. She does it to make her audiences believe her."

"You saw them, they already believe her," Kildy said. "And if that's what she's doing, why isn't it on the Berkeley videotape?"

"It isn't?"

She shook her head. "I watched it six times. Nothing."

"And you're sure your publicist's ex-boyfriend's girlfriend really saw it? That you weren't leading her when you asked her questions?"

"I'm sure," she said indignantly. "Besides, I asked my mother."

"She was there, too?"

"No, but two of her friends were, and one of them knew someone who saw the Seattle seminar. They all said basically the same thing, except the part about it making them believe her. In fact, one of them said, 'I think her cue cards were out of order,' and told me not to waste my money, that the person I should go see was Angelina Black Feather." She grinned at me and then went serious. "If Ariaura was doing it on purpose, why would she edit it out? And why did the emcee and the ushers look so uneasy?"

So she'd noticed that, too.

"Maybe she didn't warn them she was going to do it. Or, more likely, it's all part of the act, to make people believe it's authentic."

Kildy shook her head doubtfully. "I don't think so. I think it's something else."

"Like what? You don't think she's really channeling this guy?"

"No, of *course* not, Rob," she said indignantly. "It's just that…you say she's doing it to get publicity and bigger crowds, but as you told me, the first rule of success in the psychic business is to tell people what they want to hear, not to call them boobs. You saw the woman next to you—she was all ready to walk out, and I watched her afterwards. She didn't sign up for a private enlightenment audience, and neither did very many other people, and I heard the emcee telling someone there were lots of tickets still available for the next seminar. Last week's was sold out a month in advance. Why would she do something to hurt her business?"

"She's got to do something to up the ante, to keep the customers coming back, and this new spirit is to create buzz. You watch, next week she'll be advertising 'The Battle of the Ancients.' It's a gimmick, Kildy."

"So you don't think we should go see her again."

"*No.* That's the worst thing we could possibly do. We don't want to give her free publicity, and if she did do it to impress us, though it doesn't sound like it, we'd be playing right into her hands. If she's not, and the spirit *is* driving customers away, like you say, she'll dump it and come up with a different one. Or put herself out of business. Either way, there's no need for us to do anything. It's a non-story. You can forget all about her."

Which just goes to show you why I could never make it as a psychic. Because before the words were even out of my mouth, the office door banged open, and Ariaura roared in and gabbed me by the lapels.

"I don't know what you're doing or how you're doing it!" she screamed, "but I want you to stop it right now!"

3

*"He has a large and extremely uncommon
capacity for provocative utterance..."*

— H.L. MENCKEN —

◆ ◆ ◆

I hadn't given Ariaura's acting skills enough credit. Her portrayal of Isus might be wooden and fakey, but she gave a pretty convincing portrayal of a hopping-mad psychic.

"How *dare* you!" she shrieked. "I'll sue you for everything you own!"

She had changed out of her flowing robes and into a lilac-colored suit Kildy told me later was a Zac Posen, and her diamond-studded necklace and earrings rattled. She was practically vibrating with rage, though not the positive vibrations she'd said were necessary for the appearance of spirits.

"I just watched the video of my seminar," she shrieked, her face two inches from mine. "How *dare* you hypnotize me and make me look like a complete fool in front of—"

"Hypnotize?" Kildy said. (I was too busy trying to loosen her grip on my lapels to say anything.) "You think Rob hypnotized you?"

"Oh, don't play the innocent with me," Ariaura said, wheeling on her. "I saw you two out there in the audience today, and I know all about you and your nasty, sneering little magazine. I know you nonbelievers will stop at nothing to keep us from spreading the Higher Truth, but I didn't think you'd go this far, hypnotizing me against my will and making me say those things! Isus told me I shouldn't let you stay in the auditorium, that he sensed danger in your presence, but I said, 'No, let the unbelievers stay and experience your reality. Let them know you come from the Existence Beyond to help us, to bring us words of Higher Wisdom,' but Isus was right, you were up to no good."

She removed one hand from a lapel long enough to shake a lilac-lacquered fingernail at me. "Well, your little hypnotism scheme won't work. I've worked too hard to get where I am, and I'm not going to let a pair of narrow-minded little unbelievers like you get in my way. I have no intention—Higher Wisdom, my foot!" she snorted. "Higher Humbug is what I call it."

Kildy glanced, startled, at me.

"Oh, the trappings are a lot gaudier, I'll give you that," Ariaura said in the gravelly voice we'd heard at the seminar.

As before, the change had come without a break and in mid-sentence. One minute she had had me by the lapels, and the next she'd let go and was pacing around the room, her hands behind her back, musing, "That auditorium's a lot fancier, and it's a big improvement over a courthouse lawn, and a good forty degrees cooler." She sat down on the couch, her hands on her spread-apart knees. "And those duds she wears would make a grand worthy bow-wow of the Knights of Zoroaster look dowdy, but it's the same old line of buncombe and the same old Boobus Americanus drinking it in."

Kildy took a careful step toward my desk, reached for her handbag and did something I couldn't see, and then went back to where she'd been standing, keeping her eyes the whole time on Ariaura, who was holding forth about the seminar.

"I never saw such an assortment of slack-jawed simians in one place! Except for the fact that the yokels have to sit on the floor—*and* pay for the privilege!—it's the spitting image of a Baptist tent revival. Tell 'em what they want to hear, do a couple of parlor tricks, and then pass the collection plate. And they're still falling for it!" She stood up and began pacing again. "I knew I should've stuck around. It's just like that time in Dayton—I think it's all over and leave, and look what happens! You let the quacks and the crooks take over, like this latter-day Aimee Semple McPherson. She's no more a seer than—of allowing you to ruin everything I've worked for! I..." She looked around bewilderedly. "...what?...I..." She faltered to a stop.

I had to hand it to her. She was good. She'd switched back into her own voice without missing a beat, and then given an impressive impersonation of someone who had no idea what was going on.

She looked confusedly from me to Kildy and back. "It happened again, didn't it?" she asked, a quaver in her voice, and turned to appeal to Kildy. "He did it again, didn't he?" and began backing toward the door. *"Didn't* he?"

She pointed accusingly at me. "You keep *away* from me!" she shrieked. "And you keep away from my seminars! If you so much as *try* to come near me again, I'll get a restraining order against you!" she said and roared out, slamming the door behind her.

"Well," Kildy said after a minute. "That was interesting."

"Yes," I said, looking at the door. "Interesting."

Kildy went over to my desk and pulled the Hasaka out from behind her handbag. "I got it all," she said, taking out the disk, sticking it in the computer dock, and sitting down in front of the monitor. "There were a lot more clues this time." She began typing in commands. "There should be more than enough for us to be able to figure out who it is."

"I know who it is," I said.

Kildy stopped in mid-keystroke. "Who?"

"The High Priest of Irreverence."

"*Who?*"

"The Holy Terror from Baltimore, the Apostle of Common Sense, the scourge of Con Men, Creationists, Faith-Healers, and the Booboisie," I said. "Henry Louis Mencken."

"In brief, it is a fraud."

— H.L. MENCKEN —

♦ ♦ ♦

"H. L. Mencken?" Kildy said. "The reporter who covered the Scopes trial?" (I told you she was too good to be true.)

"But why would Ariaura channel him?" she asked after we'd checked the words and phrases we'd listed against Mencken's writings. They all checked out, from "buncombe" to "slackjawed simians" to "home of the imbecile and the ass."

"What did he mean about leaving Dayton early? Did something happen in Ohio?"

I shook my head. "Tennessee. Dayton was where the Scopes trial was held."

"And Mencken left early?"

"I don't know," I said, and went over to the bookcase to look for *The Great Monkey Trial*, "but I know it got so hot during the trial they moved it outside."

"That's what that comment about the courthouse lawn and its being forty degrees cooler meant," Kildy said.

I nodded. "It was a hundred and five degrees and ninety percent humidity the week of the trial. It's definitely Mencken. He invented the term 'Boobus Americanus.'"

"But why would Ariaura channel H.L. Mencken, Rob? He *hated* people like her, didn't he?"

"He certainly did." He'd been the bane of charlatans and quacks all through the Twenties, writing scathing columns on all kinds of scams, from faith-healing to chiropractic to creationism, railing incessantly against all forms of "hocus-pocus" and on behalf of science and rational thought.

"Then why would she channel him?" Kildy asked. "Why not somebody sympathetic to psychics, like Edgar Cayce or Madame Blavatsky?"

"Because they'd obviously be suspect. By channeling an enemy of psychics, she makes it seem more credible."

"But nobody's ever heard of him."

"You have. I have."

"But nobody else in Ariaura's audience has."

"Exactly," I said, still looking for *The Great Monkey Trial*.

"You mean you think she's doing it to impress us?"

"Obviously," I said, scanning the titles. "Why else would she have come all the way over here to give that little performance?"

"But—what about the Seattle seminar? Or the one in Berkeley?"

"Dry runs. Or she was hoping we'd hear about them and go see her. Which we did."

"I didn't," Kildy said. "I went because my publicist wanted me to."

"But you go to lots of spiritualist events, and you talk to lots of people. Your publicist was there. Even if you hadn't gone, she'd have told you about it."

"But what would be the point? You're a skeptic. You don't believe in channeling. Would she honestly think she could convince you Mencken was real?"

"Maybe," I said. "She's obviously gone to a lot of trouble to make the spirit sound like him. And think what a coup that would be. 'Skeptic Says Channeled Spirit Authentic'? Have you ever heard of Uri Geller? He made a splash back in the seventies by claiming to bend spoons with his mind. He got all kinds of attention when a pair of scientists from the Stanford Research Institute said it wasn't a trick, that he was actually doing it."

"Was he?"

"No, of course not, and eventually he was exposed as a fraud. By Johnny Carson. Geller made the mistake of going on the *Tonight Show* and doing it in front of him. He'd apparently forgotten Carson had been a magician in his early days. But the point is, he made it onto the *Tonight Show*. And what made him a celebrity was having the endorsement of reputable scientists."

"And if you endorsed Ariaura, if you said you thought it was really Mencken, she'd be a celebrity, too."

"Exactly."

"So what do we do?"

"Nothing."

"Nothing? You're not going to try to expose her as a fake?"

"Channeling isn't the same as bending spoons. There's no independently verifiable evidence." I looked at her. "It's not worth it, and we've got bigger fish to fry. Like Charles Fred. He's making *way* too much money for a medium who only charges two hundred a performance, and he has way too many hits for a cold-reader. We need to find out how he's doing it, and where the money's coming from."

"But shouldn't we at least go to Ariaura's next seminar to see if it happens again?" Kildy persisted.

"And have to explain to the *L.A. Times* reporter who just happens to be there why we're so interested in Ariaura?" I said. "And why you came back three times?"

"I suppose you're right. But what if some other skeptic endorses her? Or some English professor?"

I hadn't thought of that. Ariaura had dangled the bait at four seminars we knew of. She might have been doing it at more, and *The Skeptical Mind* was in Seattle, Carlyle Drew was in San Francisco, and there were any number of amateur skeptics who went to spiritualist events.

And they would all know who Mencken was. He was the critical thinker's favorite person, next to the Amazing Randi and Houdini. He'd not only been fearless in his attacks on superstition and fraud, he could write "like a bat out of hell." And, unlike the rest of us skeptics, people had actually listened to what he said.

I'd liked him ever since I'd read about him chatting with somebody in his office at the Baltimore *Sun* and then suddenly looking out the window, saying, "The sons of bitches are gaining on us!" and frantically beginning to type. That was how I felt about twice a day, and more than once I'd muttered to myself, "Where the hell is Mencken when we need him?"

And I'd be willing to bet there were other people who felt the same way I did, who might be seduced by Mencken's language and the fact that Ariaura was telling them exactly what they wanted to hear.

"You're right," I said. "We need to look into this, but we should send somebody else to the seminar."

"How about my publicist? She said she wanted to go again."

"No, I don't want it to be anybody connected with us."

"I know just the person," Kildy said, snatching up her cell phone. "Her name's Riata Starr. She's an actress."

With a name like that, what else could she be?

"She's between jobs right now," Kildy said, punching in a number, "and if I tell her there's likely to be a casting director there, she'll definitely do it for us."

"Does she believe in channelers?"

She looked pityingly at me. "Everyone in Hollywood believes in channelers, but it won't matter." She put the phone to her ear. "I'll put a videocam on her, and a recorder," she whispered. "And I'll tell her an undercover job would look great on her acting resume. Hello?" she said in a normal voice. "I'm trying to reach Riata Starr. Oh. No, no message."

She pushed 'end.' "She's at a casting call at Miramax." She stuck the phone in her bag, fished her keys out of its depths, and slung the bag over her shoulder. "I'm going to go out there and talk to her. I'll be back," she said and went out.

Definitely too good to be true, I thought, watching her leave, and called up a friend of mine in the police department and asked him what they had on Ariaura.

He promised he'd call me back, and while I was waiting I looked for and found *The Great Monkey Trial*. I looked up Mencken in the index and started through the references to see when Mencken had left Dayton. I doubted if he would have left before the trial was over. He'd been having the time of his life, pillorying William Jennings Bryan and the creationists. Maybe the reference was to Mencken's having left before Bryan's death. Bryan had died five days after the trial ended, presumably from a heart attack, but more likely from the humiliation he'd suffered at the hands of Clarence Darrow, who'd put him on the stand and fired questions at him about the Bible. Darrow had made him, and creationism, look ridiculous, or rather, Bryan had made himself look ridiculous. The cross-examination had been the high point of the trial, and it had killed him.

Mencken had written a deadly, unforgiving eulogy of Bryan, and he might very well have been sorry he hadn't been in at the kill, but I couldn't imagine Ariaura knowing that, even if she had taken the trouble to look up "Boobus Americanus" and "unmitigated bilge," and research Mencken's gravelly voice and explosive delivery.

Of course she might have read it. In this very book, even. I read the chapter on Bryan's death, looking for references to Mencken, but I couldn't find any. I backtracked, and there it was. And I couldn't believe it. Mencken hadn't left after the trial. When Darrow's expert witnesses had all been disallowed, he'd assumed it was all over but assorted legal technicalities and had gone back to Baltimore. He hadn't seen Darrow's withering cross-examination. He'd missed Bryan saying man wasn't a mammal, his insisting the sun could stand still without throwing the earth out of orbit. He'd definitely left too soon. And I was willing to bet he'd never forgiven himself for it.

5

*"To me, the scientific point of view is
completely satisfying, and it has been so as long
as I remember. Not once in this life have I ever
been inclined to seek a rock and refuge elsewhere."*
— H.L. MENCKEN —

◆ ◆ ◆

"But how could Ariaura know that?" Kildy said when she
got back from the casting call.

"The same way I know it. She read it in a book. Did your
friend Riata agree to go to the seminar?"

"Yes, she said she'd go. I gave her the Hasaka, but I'm worried
they might confiscate it, so I've got an appointment with this
props guy at Universal who worked on the last Bond movie to see
if he's got any ideas."

"Uh, Kildy...those gadgets James Bond uses aren't real. It's
a movie."

She shot me her Julia-Roberts-plus smile. "I said *ideas*. Oh,
and I got Riata's ticket. When I called, I asked if they were sold
out, and the guy I talked to said, 'Are you kidding?' and told me
they'd only sold about half what they usually do. Did you find out
anything about Ariaura?"

"No," I said. "I'm checking out some leads," but my friend at
the police department didn't have any dope on Ariaura, not even
a possible alibi.

43

"She's clean," he said when he finally called back the next morning. "No mail fraud, not even a parking ticket."

I couldn't find anything on her in *The Skeptical Mind* or on the Scamwatch website. It looked like she made her money the good old American way, by telling her customers a bunch of nonsense and selling them chakra charts.

I told Kildy as much when she came in, looking gorgeous in a casual shirt and jeans that had probably cost as much as *The Jaundiced Eye*'s annual budget.

"Ariaura's obviously not her real name, but so far I haven't been able to find out what it is," I said. "Did you get a James Bond secret videocam from your buddy, Q?"

"Yes," she said, setting the tote bag down. "And I have an idea for proving Ariaura's a fraud." She handed me a sheaf of papers. "Here are the transcripts of everything Mencken said. We check them against Mencken's writings, and—what?"

I was shaking my head. "This is channeling. When I wrote an exposé about Swami Vishnu Jammi's fifty-thousand-year-old entity, Yogati, using phrases like "totally awesome" and "funky" and talking about cell phones, he said he 'transliterated' Yogati's thoughts into his own words."

"Oh." Kildy bit her lip. "Rob, what about a computer match? You know, one of those things where they compare a manuscript with Shakespeare's plays to see if they were written by the same person."

"Too expensive," I said. "Besides, they're done by universities, who I doubt would want to risk their credibility by running a check on a channeler. And even if they did match, all it would prove is that it's Mencken's words, not that it's Mencken."

"Oh." She sat on the corner of my desk, swinging her long legs for a minute and then stood up, walked over to the bookcase, and began pulling down books.

"What are you doing?" I asked, going over to see what she was doing. She was holding a copy of Mencken's *Heathen Days*. "I told you," I said, "Mencken's phrases won't—"

"I'm not looking up his phrases," she said, handing me *Prejudices* and Mencken's biography. "I'm looking for questions to ask him."

"Him? He's not Mencken, Kildy. He's a concoction of Ariaura's."

"I know," she said, handing me *The Collectible Mencken*. "That's why we need to question him—I mean Ariaura. We need to ask him—her—questions like, 'What was your wife's maiden name?' and 'What was the first newspaper you worked for?' and—are any of these paperbacks on the bottom shelf here by Mencken?"

"No, they're mysteries mostly. Chandler and Hammett and James. M. Cain."

She straightened to look at the middle shelves. "Questions like, 'What did your father do for a living?'"

"He made cigars," I said. "The first newspaper he worked for wasn't the *Baltimore Sun*, it was the *Morning Herald*, and his wife's maiden name was Sarah Haardt. With a 'd' and two 'a's.' But that doesn't mean I'm Mencken."

"No," Kildy said, "but if you didn't know them, it would prove you weren't." She handed me *A Mencken Chrestomathy*. "If we ask Ariaura questions Mencken would know the answers to, and she gets them wrong, it proves she's faking."

She had a point. Ariaura had obviously researched Mencken fairly thoroughly to be able to mimic his language and mannerisms, and probably well enough to answer basic questions about his life, but she would hardly have memorized every detail. There were dozens of books about him, let alone his own work and his diaries. And *Inherit the Wind* and all the other plays and books and treatises that had been written about the Scopes trial. I'd bet there

45

were close to a hundred Mencken things in print, and that didn't include the stuff he'd written for the Baltimore *Sun*.

And if we could catch her not knowing something Mencken would know, it would be a simple way to prove conclusively that she was faking, and we could move on to the much more important question of why. *If* Ariaura would let herself be questioned.

"How do you plan to get Ariaura to agree to this?" I said. "My guess is she won't even let us in to see her."

"If she doesn't, then that's proof, too," she said imperturbably.

"All right," I said, "but forget about asking what Mencken's father did. Ask what he drank. Rye, by the way."

Kildy grabbed a notebook and started writing.

"Ask what the name of his first editor at the *Sun* was," I said, picking up *The Great Monkey Trial*. "And ask who Sue Hicks was."

"Who was she?" Kildy asked.

"He. He was one of the defense lawyers at the Scopes trial."

"Should we ask him—her what the Scopes trial was about?"

"No, too easy. Ask him..." I said, trying to think of a good question. "Ask him what he ate while he was there covering the trial, and ask him where he sat in the courtroom"

"Where he sat?"

"It's a trick question. He stood on a table in the corner. Oh, and ask where he was born."

She frowned. "Isn't that too easy? Everyone knows he's from Baltimore."

"I want to hear him say it."

"Oh,"Kildy said, nodding. "Did he have any kids?"

I shook my head. "He had a sister and two brothers. Gertrude, Charles, and August."

"Oh, good, that's not a name you'd be able to come up with just by guessing. Did he have any hobbies?"

"He played the piano. Ask about the Saturday Night Club. He and a bunch of friends got together to play music."

We worked on the questions the rest of the day and the next morning, writing them down on index cards so they could be asked out of order.

"What about some of his sayings?" Kildy asked.

"You mean like, 'Puritanism is the haunting fear that someone, somewhere, may be happy?' No. They're the easiest thing of all to memorize, and no real person speaks in aphorisms."

Kildy nodded and bent her beautiful head over the book again. I looked up Mencken's medical history—he suffered from ulcers and had had an operation on his mouth to remove his uvula—and went out and got us sandwiches for lunch and made copies of Mencken's "History of the Bathtub" and a fake handbill he'd passed out during the Scopes trial announcing "a public demonstration of healing, casting out devils, and prophesying" by a made-up evangelist. Mencken had crowed that not a single person in Dayton had spotted the fake.

Kildy looked up from her book. "Did you know Mencken dated Lillian Gish?" she asked, sounding surprised.

"Yeah. He dated a lot of actresses. He had an affair with Anita Loos and nearly married Aileen Pringle. Why?"

"I'm impressed he wasn't intimidated by the fact that they were movie stars, that's all."

I didn't know if that was directed at me or not. "Speaking of actresses," I said, "what time is Ariaura's seminar?"

"Two o'clock," she said, glancing at her watch. "It's a quarter till two right now. It should be over around four. Riata said she'd call as soon as the seminar was done."

We went back to looking through Mencken's books and his biographies, looking for details Ariaura was unlikely to have memorized. He'd loved baseball. He had stolen Gideon Bibles from hotel rooms and then given them to his friends, inscribed, "Compliments of the Author." He'd been friends with lots of writers, including Theodore Dreiser and F. Scott Fitzgerald, who'd gotten so drunk at a dinner with Mencken he'd stood up at the dinner table and pulled his pants down.

The phone rang. I reached for it, but it was Kildy's cell phone. "It's Riata," she told me, looking at the readout.

"Riata?"I glanced at my watch. It was only two-thirty. "Why isn't she in the seminar?"

Kildy shrugged and put the phone to her ear. "Riata? What's going on?...You're kidding!...Did you get it? Great...no, meet me at Spago's, like we agreed. I'll be there in half an hour."

She hit 'end,' stood up, and took out her keys, all in one graceful motion. "Ariaura did it again, only this time as soon as she started, they stopped the seminar, yanked her off-stage, and told everybody to leave. Riata got it on tape. I'm going to go pick it up. Will you be here?"

I nodded absently, trying to think of a way to ask about Mencken's two-fingered typing, and Kildy waved goodbye and went out.

If I asked "How do you write your stories?" I'd get an answer about the process of writing, but if I asked, "Do you touch-type?" Ariaura—

Kildy reappeared in the doorway, sat down, and picked up her notebook again. "What are you doing?" I asked, "I thought you were—"

She put her finger to her lips. "She's here," she mouthed, and Ariaura came in.

She was still wearing her purple robes and her stage makeup, so she must have come here straight from her seminar, but she didn't roar in angrily the way she had before. She looked frightened.

"What are you doing to me?" she asked, her voice trembling, "and don't say you're not doing anything. I saw the videotape. You're—that's what I want to know, too," the gravelly voice demanded. "What the hell have you been doing? I thought you ran a magazine that worked to put a stop to the kind of bilgewater this high priestess of blather spews out. She was at it again today, calling up spirits and rooking a bunch of mysticism-besotted fools out of their cold cash, and where the hell were you? I didn't see you there, cracking heads."

"We didn't go because we didn't want to encourage her if she was—" Kildy hesitated. "We're not sure what…I mean, who we're dealing with here…" she faltered.

"Ariaura," I said firmly. "You pretend to channel spirits from the astral plane for a living. Why should we believe you're not pretending to channel H.L. Mencken?"

"Pretending?" she said, sounding surprised. "You think I'm something that two-bit Jezebel's confabulating?" She sat down heavily in the chair in front of my desk and grinned wryly at me. "You're absolutely right. I wouldn't believe it either. A skeptic after my own heart."

"Yes," I said. "And as a skeptic, I need to have some proof you're who you say you are."

"Fair enough. What kind of proof?"

"We want to ask you some questions," Kildy said.

Ariaura slapped her knees. "Fire away."

"All right," I said. "Since you mentioned fires, when was the Baltimore fire?"

"Aught-four," he said promptly. "February. Cold as hell." She grinned. "Best time I ever had."

Kildy glanced at me. "What did your father drink:" she asked. "Rye."

49

"What did you drink?" I asked.

"From 1919 on, whatever I could get."

"Where are you from?" Kildy asked.

"The most beautiful city in the world."

"Which is?" I said.

"Which *is?*" she roared, outraged. "Bawlmer!"

Kildy shot me a glance.

"What's the Saturday Night Club?" I barked.

"A drinking society," she said, "with musical accompaniment."

"What instrument did you play?"

"Piano."

"What's the Mann Act?"

"Why?" she said, winking at Kildy. "You planning on taking her across state lines? Is she underage?"

I ignored that. "If you're really Mencken, you hate charlatans, so why have you inhabited Ariaura's body?"

"Why do people go to zoos?"

She was good, I had to give her that. And fast. She spat out answers as fast as I could ask questions about the *Sun* and the *Smart Set* and Williams Jennings Bryan.

"Why did you go to Dayton?"

"To see a three-ring circus. And stir up the animals."

"What did you take with you?"

"A typewriter and four quarts of Scotch. I should have taken a fan. It was hotter than the seventh circle of hell, with the same company."

"What did you eat while you were there?" Kildy asked.

"Fried chicken and tomatoes. At every meal. Even breakfast."

I handed him the bogus evangelist handbill Mencken had handed out at the Scopes trial. "What's this?"

She looked at it, turned it over, looked at the other side. "It appears to be some sort of circular."

And there's all the proof we need, I thought smugly. Mencken would have recognized that instantly. "Do you know who wrote this handbill?" I started to ask and thought better of it. The question itself might give the answer away. And better not use the word "handbill."

"Do you know the event this circular describes?" I asked instead.

"I'm afraid I can't answer that," she said.

Then you're not Mencken, I thought. I shot a triumphant glance at Kildy.

"But I would be glad to," Ariaura said, "if you would be so good as to read what is written on it to me."

She handed the handbill back to me, and I stood there looking at it and then at her and then at it again.

"What is it, Rob?" Kildy said. "What's wrong?"

"Nothing," I said. "Never mind about the circular. What was your first published news story about?"

"A stolen horse and buggy," she said and proceeded to tell the whole story, but I wasn't listening.

He didn't know who the handbill was about, I thought, because he couldn't read. Because he'd had an aphasic stroke in 1948 that had left him unable to read and write.

6

"I had a nice clean place to stay, madam,
and I left it to come here."

— *INHERIT THE WIND* —

◆ ◆ ◆

"It doesn't prove anything," I told Kildy after Ariaura was gone. She'd come out of her Mencken act abruptly after I'd asked her what street she lived on in Baltimore, looked bewilderedly at me and then Kildy, and bolted without a word. "Ariaura could have found out about Mencken's stroke the same way I did," I said, "by reading it in a book."

"Then why did you go white like that?" Kildy said. "I thought you were going to pass out. And why wouldn't she just answer the question? She knew the answers to all the others."

"Probably she didn't know that one and that was her fallback response," I said. "It caught me off-guard, that's all. I was expecting her to have memorized pat answers, not—"

"Exactly," Kildy cut in. "Somebody faking it would have said they had an aphasic stroke if you asked them a direct question about it, but they wouldn't have...and that wasn't the only instance. When you asked him about the Baltimore fire, he said it was the best time he'd ever had. Someone faking it would have told you what buildings burned or how horrible it was."

And he'd said, not "1904" or "oh-four," but "aught—four." Nobody talked like that nowadays, and it wasn't something that would have been in Mencken's writings. It was something people said, not wrote, and Ariaura couldn't possibly—

"It doesn't prove he's Mencken," I said and realized I was saying "he." And shouting. I lowered my voice. "It's a very clever trick, that's all. And just because we don't know how the trick's being done doesn't mean it's not a trick. She could have been coached in the part, *including* telling her how to pretend she can't read if she's confronted with anything written, or she could be hooked up to somebody with a computer."

"I looked. She wasn't wearing an earpiece, and if somebody was looking up the answers and feeding them to her, she'd be slower answering them, wouldn't she?"

"Not necessarily. She might have a photographic memory."

"But then wouldn't she be doing a mind-reading act instead of channeling?"

"Maybe she did. We don't know what she was doing before Salem," I said, but Kildy was right. Someone with a photographic memory could make a killing as a fortuneteller or a medium, and there were no signs of a photographic memory in Ariaura's channeling act—she spoke only in generalities.

"Or she might be coming up with the answers some other way," I said.

"What if she isn't, Rob? What if she's really channeling the spirit of Mencken?"

"Kildy, channels are fakes. There are no spirits, no sympathetic vibrations, no astral plane."

"I know," she said, "but his answers were so—" She shook her head. "And there's something about him, his voice and the way he moves—"

"It's called acting."

"But Ariaura's a terrible actress. You saw her do Isus."

"All right," I said. "Let's suppose for a minute it is Mencken, and that instead of being in the family plot in Louden Park Cemetery, his spirit's floating in the ether somewhere, why would he come back at this particular moment? Why didn't he come back when Uri Geller was bending spoons all over the place, or when Shirley MacLaine was on every talk show in the universe? Why didn't he come back in the fifties when Virginia Tighe was claiming to be Bridey Murphy?"

"I don't know," Kildy admitted.

"And why would he choose to make his appearance through the 'channel' of a third-rate mountebank like Ariaura? He *hated* charlatans like her."

"Maybe that's why he came back, because people like her are still around and he hadn't finished what he set out to do. You heard him—he said he left too early."

"He was talking about the Scopes trial."

"Maybe not. You heard him, he said 'You let the quacks and the crooks take over.' Or maybe—" she stopped.

"Maybe what?"

"Maybe he came back to help you, Rob. That time you were so frustrated over Charles Fred, I heard you say, 'Where the hell is H.L. Mencken when we need him?' Maybe he heard you."

"And decided to come all the way back from an astral plane that doesn't exist to help a skeptic nobody's ever heard of."

"It's not *that* inconceivable that someone would be interested in you," Kildy said. "I…I mean, the work you're doing is really important, and Mencken—"

"*Kildy,*" I said. "I don't believe this."

"I don't either—I just…You have to admit, it's a very convincing illusion."

"Yes, so was the Fox Sisters' table-rapping and Virginia Tighe's past life as an Irish washerwoman in 1880s Dublin, but there was a logical explanation for both of them, and it may not even be that complicated. The details Bridey Murphy knew all turned out to have come from Virginia Tighe's Irish nanny. The Fox Sisters were cracking their *toes,* for God's sake."

"You're right," Kildy said, but she didn't sound completely convinced, and that worried me. If Ariaura's Mencken imitation could fool Kildy, it could fool anybody, and "I'm sure it's a trick. I just don't know how she's doing it," wasn't going to cut it when the networks called me for a statement. I had to figure this out fast.

"Ariaura has to be getting her information about Mencken from someplace," I said. "We need to find out where. We need to check with bookstores and the library. And the internet," I said, hoping that wasn't what she was using. It would take forever to find out what sites she'd visited.

"What do you want me to do?" Kildy asked.

"I want you to go through the transcripts like you suggested and find out where the quotes came from so we'll know the particular works we're dealing with," I told her. "And I want you to talk to your publicist and anybody else who's been to the seminars and find out if any of them had a private enlightenment audience with Ariaura. I want to know what goes on in them. Is she using Mencken for some purpose we don't know about? See if you can find out."

"I could ask Riata to get one," she suggested.

"That's a good idea," I said.

"What about questions? Do you want me to try to come up with some harder ones than the ones we asked him—I mean, her?"

I shook my head. "Asking harder questions won't help. If she's got a photographic memory, she'll know anything we throw at her, and if she doesn't, and we ask her some obscure question about one of the reporters Mencken worked with at the *Morning*

Herald, or one of his *Smart Set* essays, she can say she doesn't remember, and it won't prove anything. If you asked me what was in articles I wrote for *The Jaundiced Eye* five years ago, I couldn't remember either."

"I'm not talking about facts and figures, Rob," Kildy said. "I'm talking about the kinds of things people don't forget, like the first time Mencken met Sara."

I thought of the first time I met Kildy, looking up from my desk to see her standing there, with her blonde hair and that movie-star smile. Unforgettable was the word, all right.

"Or how his mother died," Kildy was saying, "or how he found out about the Baltimore fire. The paper called him and woke him out of a sound sleep. There's no way you could forget that, or the name of a dog you had as a kid, or the nickname the other kids called you in grade school."

Nickname. That triggered something. Something Ariaura wouldn't know. About a baby. Had Mencken had a nickname when he was a baby? No, that wasn't it—

"Or what he got for Christmas when he was ten," Kildy said. "We need to find a question Mencken would absolutely know the answer to, and if he doesn't, it proves it's Ariaura."

"And if he does, it still doesn't prove it's Mencken. Right?"

"I'll go talk to Riata about getting a private audience," she said, stuffed the transcripts in her tote, and put on her sunglasses. "And I'll pick up the videotape. I'll see you tomorrow morning."

"Right, Kildy?" I insisted.

"Right," she said, her hand on the door. "I guess."

*"In the highest confidence there is always
a flavor of doubt—a feeling, half instinctive
and half logical, that, after all, the scoundrel
may have something up his sleeve."*

— H.L. MENCKEN —

◆ ◆ ◆

A fter Kildy left, I called up a computer-hacker friend of mine
and put him to work on the problem and then phoned a
guy I knew in the English department at UCLA.

"Inquiries about Mencken?" he said. "Not that I know of, Rob.
You might try the journalism department."

The guy at the journalism department said, "Who?" and,
when I explained, suggested I call Johns Hopkins in Baltimore.

And what had I been thinking? Kildy said Ariaura had started
doing Mencken in Seattle. I needed to be checking there, or in Salem
or—where had she gone after that? Sedona. I spent the rest of the
day (and evening) calling bookstores and reference librarians in all
three places. Five of them responded "Who?" and all of them asked
me how to spell 'Mencken,' which might or might not mean they
hadn't heard the name lately, and only seven of the thirty bookstores
stocked any books on him. Half of those were the latest Mencken
biography, which for an excited moment I thought might have
answered the question, "Why Mencken?"—the title of it was *Skeptic*

and Prophet—but it had only been out two weeks. None of the bookstores could give me any information on orders or recent purchases, and the public libraries couldn't give me any information at all.

I tried their electronic card catalogues, but they only showed currently checked-out books. I called up the L.A. Public Library's catalogue. It showed four Mencken titles checked out, all from the Beverly Hills branch.

"Which looks promising," I told Kildy when she came in the next morning.

"No, it doesn't," she said. "I'm the one who checked them out, to compare the transcripts against." She pulled a sheaf of papers out of her designer tote. "I need to talk to you about the transcripts. I found something interesting. I know," she said, anticipating my objection, "you said all it proved was that Ariaura—"

"Or whoever's feeding this stuff to her."

She acknowledged that with a nod, "—all it proved was that whoever was doing it was reading Mencken, and I agree, but you'd expect her to quote him back verbatim, wouldn't you?"

"Yes," I said, thinking of Randall Mars's Lincoln and his "Four-score and seven…"

"But she doesn't. Look, here's what she said when we asked him about William Jennings Bryan: 'Bryan! I don't even want to hear that mangey old mountebank's name mentioned. That scoundrel had a malignant hatred of science and sense.'"

"And he didn't say that?"

"Yes and no. Mencken called him a 'walking malignancy' and said he was 'mangey and fleabitten' and had 'an almost pathological hatred of all learning.' And the rest of the answers, and the things she said at the seminars, are like that, too."

"So she mixed and matched his phrases," I said, but what she'd found was disturbing. Someone trying to pull off an impersonation would stick to the script, since any deviations from Mencken's actual words could be used as proof it wasn't him.

And the annotated list Kildy handed me was troubling in another way. The phrases hadn't been taken from one or two sources. They were from all over the map—"complete hooey" from *Minority Report*, "buncombe" from *The New Republic*, "as truthful as Lydia Pinkham's Vegetable Compound" from an article on pedagogy in the *Sun*.

"Could they all have been in a Mencken biography?'"

She shook her head. "I checked. I found a couple of sources that had several of them, but no one source that had them all."

"That doesn't mean there isn't one," I said and changed the subject. "Was your friend able to get a private audience with Ariaura?"

"Yes," she said, glancing at her watch. "I have to go meet her in a few minutes. She also got tickets to the seminar Saturday. They didn't cancel it like I thought they would, but they did cancel a local radio interview she was supposed to do last night, and the week-long spiritual immersion she had scheduled for next week."

"Did she give you the recording of Ariaura's last seminar?"

"No, she'd left it at home. She said she'd bring it when we meet before her private audience. She said she got some really good footage of the emcee. She swears from the way he looked that he's not in on the scam. And there's something else. I called Judy Helzberg, who goes to every psychic event there is— Remember? I interviewed her when we did the piece on shamanic astrologers—And she said Ariaura called her and asked her for Wilson Amboy's number."

"Wilson Amboy?"

"Beverly Hills psychiatrist."

"It's all part of the illusion," I said, but even I sounded a little doubtful. It was an awfully good deception for a third-rate channeler like Ariaura. There's somebody else in on it, I thought, and not just somebody feeding her answers. A partner. A mastermind.

After Kildy left I called Marty Rumboldt and asked him if Ariaura had had a partner in Salem. "Not that I know of," he said. "Prentiss just did a study on witchcraft in Salem. She might know somebody who would know. Hang on. Hey, Prentiss!" I could hear him call. "Jamie!"

Jamie, I thought. That had been James M. Cain's nickname, and Mencken had been good friends with him. Where had I read that?

"She said to call Madame Orima," Marty said, getting back on the phone, and gave me the number.

I started to dial it and then stopped and looked up "Cain, James M." in Mencken's biography. It said he and Mencken had worked on the *Baltimore Sun* together, that they had been good friends, that Mencken had helped him get his first story collection published: *The Baby in the Icebox*.

I went over to the bookcase, squatted down, and started through the row of paperbacks on the bottom shelf...Chandler, Hammett...It had a red cover, with a picture of a baby in a high chair and a...Chandler, Cain...

But no red. I scanned the titles—*Double Indemnity, The Postman Always Rings Twice*...Here it was, stuck behind *Mildred Pierce* and not red at all. *The Baby in the Icebox*. It was a lurid orange and yellow, and had pictures of a baby in its mother's arms and a cigarette-smoking lug in front of a gas station. I hoped I remembered the inside better than the outside.

I did. The introduction was by Roy Hoopes, and it was not only a Penguin edition, but one that had been out of print for at least twenty years. Even if Ariaura's researcher had bothered to check out Cain, it would hardly be this edition.

And the introduction was full of stuff about Cain that was perfect—the fact that everyone who knew him called him Jamie, the fact that he'd spent a summer in a tuberculosis sanitarium and hated Baltimore, Mencken's favorite place.

Some of the information was in the Mencken books—Mencken's introducing him to Alfred A. Knopf, who'd published that first collection, the *Sun* connection, their rivalry over movie star Aileen Pringle.

But most of the facts in the introduction weren't, and they were exactly the kind of thing a friend would know. And Ariaura wouldn't, because they were details about Cain's life, not Mencken's. Even a mastermind wouldn't have memorized every detail of Cain's life or those of Mencken's other famous friends. If there wasn't anything here I could use, there might be something in Dreiser's biography, or F. Scott Fitzgerald's. Or Lillian Gish's.

But there was plenty here, like the fact that his brother Boydie had died in a tragic accident after the Armistice, and his statement that all his writing was modeled on *Alice in Wonderland*. That was something no one would ever guess from reading Cain's books, which were all full of crimes and murderers and beautiful, calculating women who seduced the hero into helping her with a scam and then turned out to be working a scam of her own.

Not exactly the kind of thing Ariaura would read, and definitely the kind of thing Mencken would have. He'd bought "The Baby in the Icebox" for the *American Mercury* and told Cain it was one of the best things he'd ever written. Which meant it would make a perfect source for a question, and I knew just what to ask. To anyone who hadn't heard of the story, the question wouldn't even make sense. Only somebody who'd read the story would know the answer. Like Mencken.

And if Ariaura knew it, I'd—what? Believe she was actually channeling Mencken?

Right. And Charles Fred was really talking to the dead and Uri Geller was really bending spoons.

It was a trick, that was all. She had a photographic memory, or somebody was feeding her the answers.

Feeding her the answers.

I thought suddenly of Kildy, saying, "Who *was* Sue Hicks?" of her insisting I go with her to see Ariaura, of her saying, "But why would Ariaura channel a spirit who yells at her audiences?"

I looked down at the orange-and-yellow paperback in my hand. "A beautiful, calculating woman who seduces the hero into helping her with a scam," I murmured, and thought about Ariaura's movie-star-handsome ushers and about scantily-clad Victorian spirits and about Sir William Crookes.

Sex. Get the chump emotionally involved and he won't see the wires. It was the oldest trick in the book.

I'd said Ariaura wasn't smart enough to pull off such a complicated scam, and she wasn't. But Kildy was. So you get her on the inside where she can see the shelf full of Mencken books, where she can hear the chump mutter, "Where the hell is Mencken when we need him?" You get the chump to trust her, and if he falls in love with her, so much the better. It'll keep him off-balance and he won't get suspicious.

And it all fit. It was Kildy who'd set up the contact—I never did channelers, and Kildy knew that. It was Kildy who'd said we couldn't go incognito, Kildy who'd said to bring the Sony, knowing it would be confiscated, Kildy who'd taken a taxi to the seminar instead of coming in her Jaguar so she'd be at the office when Ariaura came roaring in.

But she'd gotten the whole thing on tape. And she hadn't had any idea who the spirit was. I was the one who'd figured out it was Mencken.

With Kildy feeding me clues from the seminar she'd gone to before, and I only had her word that Ariaura had channeled him that time. And that it had happened in Berkeley and Seattle. And that the tapes had been edited.

And she was the one who'd kept telling me it was really Mencken, the one who'd come up with the idea of asking him questions that would prove it—questions I'd conveniently told her the answers to—the one who'd suggested a friend of hers go to the seminar and videotape it, a videotape I'd never seen. I wondered if it—or Riata—even existed.

The whole thing, from beginning to end, had been a set-up. And I had never tumbled to it. Because I'd been too busy looking at her legs and her hair and that smile. Just like Crookes.

I don't believe it, I thought. Not Kildy, who'd worked side-by-side with me for nearly a year, who'd stolen chicken guts and pre-tended to be hypnotized and let Jean-Piette cleanse her aura, who'd come to work for me in the first place because she hated scam-artists like Ariaura.

Right. Who'd come to work for a two-bit magazine when she could have been getting five million a movie and dating Viggo Mortenson. Who'd been willing to give up premieres and sum-mers in Tahiti and deep massages for me. Skeptics' Rule Number Two: If it seems too good to be true, it is. And how often have you said she's a good actress?

No, I thought, every bone in my body rebelling. It can't be true.

And that's what the chump always says, isn't it, even when he's faced with the evidence? "I don't believe it. She wouldn't do that to me."

And that was the whole point—to get you to trust her, to make you believe she was on your side. Otherwise you'd have insisted on checking those tapes of Ariaura's seminars for yourself to see if they'd been edited, you'd have demanded independently verifiable evidence that Ariaura had really cancelled those seminars and asked about a psychiatrist.

Independently verifiable evidence. That's what I needed, and I knew exactly where to look.

"My mother took me to Lucius Windfire's luminescence reading," Kildy had said, and I had the guest lists for those readings. They were part of the court records, and I'd gotten them when I'd done the story on his arrest. Kildy had come to see me on May tenth and he'd only had two seminars that month.

I called up the lists for both seminars and for the two before that and typed in Kildy's name.

Nothing.

She said she went with her mother, I thought, and typed her mom's name in. Nothing. And nothing when I printed out the lists and went through them by hand, nothing when I went through the lists for March and April. And June. And no ten thousand dollar donation on any of Windfire, Inc.'s financial statements.

Half an hour later Kildy showed up smiling, beautiful, full of news."Ariaura's cancelled all the private sessions she scheduled and the rest of her tour." She leaned over my shoulder to look at what I was doing. "Did you come up with a foolproof question for Mencken?"

"No," I said, sliding *The Baby in the Icebox* under a file folder and sticking them both in a drawer. "I came up with a theory about what's going on, though."

"Really?" she said.

"Really. You know, one of my big problems all along has been Ariaura. She's just not smart enough to have come up with all this—the "aught-four" thing, the not being able to read, the going to see a psychiatrist. Which either meant she was actually channeling Mencken, or there was some other factor. And I think I've got it figured out."

"You have?"

"Yeah. Tell me what you think of this: Ariaura wants to be big. Not just seven-hundred-and-fifty a pop seminars and thirty-dollar videotapes, but *Oprah,* the *Today Show, Larry King,* the whole works. But to do that it's not enough to have audiences who believe her. She needs to have somebody with credibility say she's for real, a scientist, say, or a professional skeptic."

"Like you," she said cautiously.

"Like me. Only I don't believe in astral spirits. Or channelers. And I certainly wouldn't fall for the spirit of an ancient priest of Atlantis. It's going to have to be somebody a charlatan would never dream of channeling, somebody who'll say what I want to hear. And somebody I know a lot about so I'll recognize the clues being fed to me, somebody custom-tailored for me."

"Like H.L. Mencken," Kildy said. "But how would she have known you were a fan of Mencken's?"

"She didn't have to," I said. "That was her partner's job."

"Her part—"

"Partner, sidekick, shill, whatever you want to call it. Somebody I'd trust when she said it was important to go see some channeler."

"Let me get this straight," she said. "You think I went to Ariaura's seminar, and her imitation of Isus was so impressive I immediately became a Believer with a capital B and fell in with her nefarious scheme, whatever it is?"

"No," I said. "I think you were in it with her from the beginning, from the very first day you came to work for me."

She really was a good actress. The expression in those beautiful blue eyes looked exactly like stunned hurt. "You believe I set you up," she said wonderingly.

I shook my head. "I'm a skeptic, remember? I deal in independently verifiable evidence. Like this," I said and handed her Lucius Windfire's attendee list.

She looked at it in silence.

"Your whole story about how you found out about me was a fake, wasn't it? You didn't look up 'debunkers' in the phone book, did you? You didn't go see a luminescence therapist with your mother?"

"No."

No.

I hadn't realized till she admitted it how much I had been counting on her saying, "There must be some mistake, I was there," on her having some excuse, no matter how phony: "Did I say the fourteenth? I meant the twentieth," or "My publicist got the tickets for us. It would be in her name." Anything. Even flinging the list dramatically at me and sobbing, "I can't believe you don't trust me."

But she just stood there, looking at the incriminatory list and then at me, not a tantrum or a tear in sight.

"You concocted the whole story," I said finally.

"Yes."

I waited for her to say, "It's not the way it looks, Rob, I can explain," but she didn't say that either. She handed the list back to me and picked up her cell phone and her bag, fishing for her keys and then slinging her bag over her shoulder as casually as if she were on her way to go cover a New Moon ceremony or a tarot reading, and left.

And this was the place in the story where the private eye takes a bottle of Scotch out of his bottom drawer, pours himself a nice stiff drink, and congratulates himself on his narrow escape.

I'd almost been made a royal chump of, and Mencken (the real one, not the imitation Kildy and Ariaura had tried to pass off as him) would never have forgiven me. So good riddance. And what I needed to do now was write up the whole sorry scam as a lesson to other skeptics for the next issue.

But I sat there a good fifteen minutes, thinking about Kildy and her exit, and knowing that, in spite of its offhandedness, I was never going to see her again.

8

"What I need is a miracle."

— *INHERIT THE WIND* —

◆ ◆ ◆

I told you I'd make a lousy psychic. The next morning Kildy walked in carrying an armload of papers and file folders. She dumped them in front of me on my desk, picked up my phone and began punching in numbers.

"What the hell do you think you're doing? And what's all this?" I said, gesturing at the stack of papers.

"Independently verifiable evidence," she said, still punching in numbers, and put the phone to her ear. "Hello, this is Kildy Ross. I need to speak to Ariaura." There was a pause. "She's not taking calls? All right, tell her I'm at the *Jaundiced Eye* office, and I need to speak to her as soon as possible. Tell her it's urgent. Thank you." She hung up.

"What the hell do you think you're doing, calling Ariaura on my phone?" I said.

"I wasn't," she said. "I was calling Mencken." She pulled a file out of the middle of the stack. "I'm sorry it took me so long. Getting Ariaura's phone records was harder than I thought."

"Ariaura's phone records?"

"Yeah. Going back four years," she said, pulling a file folder out of the middle of the stack and handing it to me.

I opened it up. "How did you get her phone records?"

"I know this computer guy at Pixar. We should do an issue on how easy it is to get hold of private information and how mediums are using it to convince their people they're talking to their dead relatives," she said, fishing through the stack for another folder. "And here are my phone records." She handed it to me. "The cell's on top, and then my home number and my car phone. And my mom's. And my publicist's cell phone."

"Your publicist's cell—?"

She nodded. "In case you think I used her phone to call Ariaura. She doesn't have a regular phone, just a cell. And here are my dad's and my stepmother's. I can get my other stepmothers', too, but it'll take a couple more days, and Ariaura's big seminar is tonight."

She handed me more files. "This is a list of all my trips—airline tickets, hotel bills, rental car records. Credit card bills, with annotations," she said, and went over to her tote bag and pulled out three fat Italian-leather notebooks with a bunch of post-its sticking out the sides. "These are my dayplanners, with notes as to what the abbreviations mean, and my publicist's log."

"And this is supposed to prove you were at Lucius Windfire's luminescence reading with your mother?"

"No, Rob, I told you, I lied about the seminar," she said, looking earnestly through the stack, folder by folder. "These are to prove I didn't call Ariaura, that she didn't call me, that I wasn't in Seattle or Eugene or any of the other cities she was in, and never went to Salem." She pulled a folder out of the pile and began handing items to me. "Here's the program for Yogi Magaputra's matinee performance for May nineteenth. I couldn't find the ticket stubs and I didn't buy the tickets, the studio did, but here's a receipt for the champagne cocktail I had at intermission. See? It's got the date and it was at the Roosevelt, and here's a schedule of Magaputra's performances, showing he was at the Roosevelt on that day. And a flyer for the next session they gave out as we left."

I had one of those flyers in my file on mediums, and I was pretty sure I'd been at that séance. I'd gone to three, working on a piece on his use of funeral home records to obtain information on his victims' dead relatives. I'd never published it—he'd been arrested on tax evasion charges before I finished it. I looked questioningly at Kildy.

"I was there researching a movie I was thinking about doing," Kildy said, "a comedy about a medium. It was called *Medium Rare*. Here's the screenplay." She handed me a thick bound manuscript. "I wouldn't read the whole thing. It's terrible. Anyway, I saw you there, talking to this guy with hair transplants—"

Magaputra's personal manager, who I'd suspected was feeding him info from the audience. I'd been trying to see if I could spot his concealed mike.

"I saw you talking to him, and I thought you looked—"

"Gullible?"

Her jaw tightened. "No. Interesting. Cute. Not the kind of guy I expected to see at one of the yogi's séances. I asked who you were, and somebody said you were a professional skeptic, and I thought, well, thank goodness! Magaputra was *patently* fake, and everyone was buying it, lock, stock, and barrel."

"Including your mother," I said.

"No, I made that up, too. My mother's even more of a skeptic than I am, especially after being married to my father. She's partly why I was interested—she's always after me to date guys from outside the movie business—so I bought a copy of *The Jaundiced Eye* and got your address and came to see you."

"And lied."

"Yes," she said. "It was a dumb thing to do. I knew it as soon as you started talking about how you shouldn't take anything anyone tells you on faith and how important independently verifiable evidence is, but I was afraid if I told you I was doing research for a movie you wouldn't want me tagging along, and if I told you I was attracted to you, you wouldn't believe me. You'd think it was a reality show or some kind of Hollywood fad thing everybody was doing right then, like opening a boutique or knitting or checking into Betty Ford."

"And you fully intended to tell me," I said, "you were just waiting for the right moment. In fact, you were all set to when Ariaura came along—"

"You don't have to be sarcastic," she said. "I thought if I went to work for you and you got to know me, you might stop thinking of me as a movie star and ask me out—"

"And incidentally pick up some good acting tips for your medium movie."

"Yes," she said angrily. "If you want to know the truth, I also thought if I kept going to those stupid past-life regression sessions and covens and soul retrieval circles, I might get over the stupid crush I had on you, but the better I got to know you, the worse it got." She looked up at me. "I know you don't believe me, but I didn't set you up. I'd never seen Ariaura before I went to that first seminar with my publicist, and I'm not in any kind of scam with her. And that story I told you the first day is the only thing I've ever lied to you about. Everything else I told you—about hating psychics and Ben Affleck and wanting to get out of the movie business and wanting to help you debunk charlatans and loathing the idea of ending up in rehab or in *The Hulk IV*—was true." She rummaged in the pile and pulled out an olive green-covered script. "They really did offer me the part."

"Of the Hulk?"

"No," she said and held the script out to me. "Of the love interest."

She looked up at me with those blue eyes of hers, and if anything had ever been too good to be true, it was Kildy, standing there with that bilious green script and the office's fluorescent light on her golden hair. I had always wondered how all those chumps sitting around sÈance tables and squatting on lilac-colored cushions could believe such obvious nonsense. Well, now I knew.

Because standing there right then, knowing it all had to be a scam, that the Hulk script and the credit card bills and the phone bills didn't prove a thing, that they could easily have been faked and I was nothing more than a prize chump being set up for the big finale by a couple of pros, I still wanted to believe it. And not just the researching-a-movie alibi, but the whole thing—that H.L. Mencken had come back from the grave, that he was here to help me crusade against charlatans, that if I grabbed the wrist holding that script and pulled Kildy toward me and kissed her, we would live happily ever after.

And no wonder Mencken, railing against creationists and chiropractic and Mary Baker Eddy, hadn't gotten anywhere. What chance do facts and reason possibly have against what people desperately need to believe?

Only Mencken hadn't come back. A third-rate channeler was only pretending to be him, and Kildy's protests of love, much as I wanted to hear them, were the oldest trick in the book.

"Nice try," I said.

"But you don't believe me," she said bleakly, and Ariaura walked in.

"I got your message," she said to Kildy in Mencken's gravelly voice. "I came as soon as I could." She plunked down in a chair facing me. "Those goons of Ariaura's—"

"You can knock off the voices, Ariaura," I said. "The jig, as Mencken would say, is up."

Ariaura looked inquiringly at Kildy.

"Rob thinks Ariaura's a fake," Kildy said.

Ariaura switched her gaze to me. "You just figured that out? Of course she's a fake, she's a bamboozling mounteback, an oleaginous—"

"He thinks you're not real," Kildy said. "He thinks you're just a voice Ariaura does, like Isus, that your disrupting her seminars is a trick to convince him she's an authentic channeler, and he thinks I'm in on the plot with you, that I helped you set him up."

Here it comes, I thought. Shocked outrage. Affronted innocence. Kildy's a total stranger, I've never seen her before in my life!

"He thinks that you—?" Ariaura hooted and banged the arms of the chair with glee. "Doesn't the poor fish know you're in love with him?"

"He thinks that's part of the scam," Kildy said earnestly. "The only way he'll believe I am is if he believes there *isn't* no one, if he believes you're really Mencken."

"Well, then," Ariaura said and grinned, "I guess we'll have to convince him." He slapped his knees and turned expectantly to me. "What do you want to know, sir? I was born in 1880 at nine p.m., right before the police went out and raided ten or twenty saloons, and went to work at the *Morning Herald* at the tender age of eighteen—"

"Where you laid siege to the editor Max Ways for four straight weeks before he gave you an assignment," I said, "but my knowing that doesn't any more make me Henry Lawrence Mencken than it does you."

"Henry *Louis*," Ariaura said, "after an uncle of mine who died when he was a baby. All right, you set the questions."

"It's not that simple," Kildy said. She pulled a chair up in front of Ariaura and sat down, facing her. She took both hands in hers. "To prove you're Mencken you can't just answer questions. The skeptic's first rule is: 'Extraordinary claims require extraordinary evidence.' You've got to do something extraordinary."

"And independently verifiable," I said.

"Extraordinary," Ariaura said, looking at Kildy. "I presume you're not talking about handling snakes. Or speaking in tongues."

"No," I said.

"The problem is, if you prove you're Mencken," Kildy said earnestly, "then you're also proving that Ariaura's really channeling astral spirits, which means she's not—"

"—the papuliferous poser I know her to be."

"Exactly," Kildy said, "and her career will skyrocket."

"Along with that of every other channeler and psychic and medium out there," I said.

"Rob's put his entire life into trying to debunk these people," Kildy said. "If you prove Ariaura's really channeling—"

"The noble calling of skepticism will be dealt a heavy blow," Ariaura said thoughtfully, "hardly the outcome a man like Mencken would want. So the only way I can prove who I am is to keep silent and go back to where I came from."

Kildy nodded.

"But I came to try and stop her. If I return to the ether, Ariaura will go right back to spreading her pernicious astral-plane-Higher-Wisdom hokum and bilking her benighted audiences out of their cash."

Kildy nodded again. "She might even pretend she's channeling you."

"*Pretend!*" Ariaura said, outraged. "I won't allow it! I'll—" and then stopped. "But if I speak out, I'm proving the very thing I'm trying to debunk. And if I don't—"

"Rob will never trust me again," Kildy said.

"So," Ariaura said, "it's—"

A catch-22, I thought, and then, if she says that I've got her—the book wasn't written till 1961, five years after Mencken had died. And "catch-22" was the kind of thing, unlike "Bible belt" or "booboisie," that even Kildy wouldn't have thought of, it had become such an ingrained part of the language. I listened, waiting for Ariaura to say it.

"—a conundrum," she said.

"A what?" Kildy said.

"A puzzle with no solution, a hand there's no way to win, a hellacious dilemma."

"You're saying it's impossible," Kildy said hopelessly.

Ariaura shook her head."I've had tougher assignments than this. There's bound to be something—" She turned to me."She said something about 'the skeptic's first rule.'Are there any others?"

"Yes," I said. "If it seems too good to be true, it is."

"And 'by their fruits shall ye know them,'" Kildy said. "It's from the Bible."

"The Bible..." Ariaura said, narrowing her eyes thoughtfully. "The Bible...how much time have we got? When's Ariaura's next show?"

"Tonight," Kildy said, "but she cancelled the last one. What if she—"

"What time?" Ariaura cut in.

"Eight o'clock."

"Eight o'clock," she repeated, and made a motion toward her mid-section for all the world like she was reaching for a pocket watch. "You two be out there, front row center."

"What are you doing to do?" Kildy asked hopefully.

"I dunno," Ariaura said. "Sometimes you don't have to do a damned thing—they do it to themselves. Look at that High Muckitymuck of Hot Air, Bryan." She laughed. "Either of you know where I can get some rope?" She didn't wait for an answer. "—I'd better get on it. There's only a couple hours to deadline—" She slapped her knees. "Front row center," she said to Kildy. "Eight o'clock."

"What if she won't let us in?" Kildy asked. "Ariaura said he was going to get a restraining order against—"

"She'll let you in. Eight o'clock."

Kildy nodded. "I'll be there, but I don't know if Rob—"

"Oh, I wouldn't miss this for the world," I said.

Ariaura ignored my tone. "Bring a notebook," she ordered. "And in the meantime, you'd better get busy on your charlatan debunking. The sons of bitches are gaining on us."

*"One sits through long sessions...and then suddenly
there comes a show so gaudy and hilarious, so melodra-
matic and obscene, so unimaginably exhilarating and
preposterous that one lives a gorgeous year in an hour."*
— H.L. MENCKEN —

◆ ◆ ◆

An hour later a messenger showed up with a manila envelope.
In it was a square vellum envelope sealed with pink sealing
wax and embossed with Isus's hieroglyphs. Inside were a lilac card
printed in silver with "The pleasure of your company is requested..." and two tickets to the seminar. "Is the invitation signed?"
Kildy asked. She'd refused to leave after Ariaura'd departed, still
acting the part of Mencken. "I'm staying right here with you till the
seminar," she'd said, perching herself on my desk. "It's the only way
I can prove I'm not off somewhere with Ariaura cooking up some
trick. And here's my phone," she'd handed me her cell phone, "so
you won't think I'm sending her secret messages via text-message
or something. Do you want to check me to see if I'm wired?"

"No."

"Do you need any help?" she'd asked, picking up a pile of
proofs. "Do you want me to go over these, or am I fired?"

"I'll let you know after the seminar."

She'd given me a Julia-Roberts radiant smile and retreated to
the far end of the office with the proofs, and I'd called up Charles

Fred's file and started through it, looking for leads and trying not to think about Ariaura's parting shot.

I was positive I'd never told Kildy that story, and it wasn't in Daniels's biography, or Hobson's. The only place I'd ever seen it was in an article in the *Atlantic Monthly*. I looked it up in Bartlett's, but it wasn't there. I googled "Mencken—bitches." Nothing.

Which didn't prove anything. Ariaura—or Kildy—could have read it in the *Atlantic Monthly* just like I had. And since when had H.L. Mencken looked to the Bible for inspiration? That remark alone proved it wasn't Mencken, didn't it? On the other hand, he hadn't said "catch-22," although "conundrum" wasn't nearly as precise a word. And he hadn't said William Jennings Bryan, he'd said "that High Muckitymuck of Hot Air, Bryan," which I hadn't read anywhere, but which sounded like something he would have put in that scathing eulogy he'd written of Bryan.

And this wasn't going anywhere. There was nothing, short of a heretofore undiscovered manuscript or a will in his handwriting leaving everything to Lillian Gish—no, that wouldn't work. The aphasic stroke, remember?—that would prove it was Mencken. And both of those could be faked, too.

And there wasn't anything that could do what Kildy had told him—correction, had told Ariaura she had to do: prove he was real without proving Ariaura was legit. Which she clearly wasn't.

I got out Ariaura's transcripts and read through them, looking for I wasn't sure what, until the tickets came.

"Is the card signed?" Kildy asked again.

"No," I said and handed it to her.

"'The pleasure of your company is requested...' is printed on," she said, turning the invitation over to look at the back. "What about the address on the envelope?"

"There isn't one," I said, seeing where she was going with this. "But just because it's not handwritten, that doesn't prove it's from Mencken."

"I know. 'Extraordinary claims,' but at least it's consistent with its being Mencken."

"It's also consistent with the two of you trying to convince me it's Mencken so I'll go to that seminar tonight."

"You think it's a trap?" Kildy said.

"Yes," I said, but standing there, staring at the tickets, I had no idea what kind. Ariaura couldn't possibly still be hoping I'd stand up and shout, "By George, she's the real thing! She's channeling Mencken!" no matter what anecdote she quoted. I wondered if her lawyers might be intending to slap me with a restraining order or a subpoena when I walked in, but that made no sense. She knew my address—she'd been here this very afternoon, and I'd been here most of the past two days. Besides, if she had me arrested, the press would be clamoring to talk to me, and she wouldn't want me voicing my suspicions of a con game to the L.A. *Times*.

When Kildy and I left for the seminar an hour and a half later (on our way out, I'd pretended I forgot my keys and left Kildy standing in the hall while I went back in, bound *The Baby in the Icebox* with Scotch tape, and hid it down behind the bookcase) I still hadn't come up with a plausible theory, and the Santa Monica Hilton, where the seminar was being held, didn't yield any clues.

It had the same "Believe and It Will Happen" banner, the same Tom Cruise-ish bodyguards, the same security check. They confiscated my Olympus and my digital recorder and Kildy's Hasaka (and asked for her autograph), and we went through the same crystal/pyramid/amulet-crammed waiting area into the same lilac-and-rose draped ballroom. With the same hard, bare floor.

"Oh, I forgot to bring pillows, I'm sorry," Kildy said and started toward the ushers and stacks of lilac-plastic cushions at the rear. Halfway there she turned around and came back. "I don't want to have had an opportunity to send some kind of secret message to Ariaura," she said. "If you want to come with me…"

I shook my head. "The floor'll be good," I said, lowering myself to the floor. "It may actually keep me in touch with reality."

Kildy sat down effortlessly beside me, opened her bag, and fumbled in it for her mirror. I looked around. The crowd seemed a little sparser, and somewhere behind us, I heard a woman say, "It was so bizarre. Romtha never did anything like that. I wonder if she's drinking."

The lights went pink, the music swelled, and Brad Pitt came out, went through the same spiel (no flash, no applause, no bathroom breaks) and the same intro (Atlantis, Oracle of Delphi, Cosmic All), and revealed Ariaura, standing at the top of the same black stairway.

She was exactly the same as she had been at that first seminar, dramatically regal in her purple robes and amulets, serene as she acknowledged the audience's applause. The events of the past few days—her roaring into my office, asking frightenedly, "What's happening? Where am I?," slapping her knees and exploding with laughter—might never have happened.

And obviously had been a fake, I thought grimly. I glanced at Kildy. She was still fishing unconcernedly in her bag.

"Welcome, Seekers after Divine Truth," Ariaura said. "We're going to have a wonderful spiritual experience together here today. It's a very special day. This is my one hundredth 'Believe and It Will Happen' seminar."

Lots of applause, which after a couple of minutes she motioned to stop.

"In honor of the anniversary, Isus and I want to do something a little different today."

More applause. I glanced at the ushers. They were looking nervously at each other, as if they expected her to start spouting Menckenese, but the voice was clearly Ariaura's and so was the Oprah-perky manner.

"My—*our*—seminars are usually pretty structured. They have to be—if the auratic vibrations aren't exactly right beforehand, the spirits cannot come, and after I've channeled, I'm physically and spiritually exhausted, so I rarely have the opportunity to just *talk* to you. But today's a special occasion. So I'd like the tech crew—" she looked up at the control booth "—to bring up the lights—"

There was a pause, as if the tech crew was debating whether to follow orders, and then the lights came up.

"Thanks, that's perfect, you can have the rest of the day off," Ariaura said. She turned to the emcee. "That goes for you, too, Ken. And my fabulous ushers—Derek, Jared, Tad—let's hear it for the great job they do."

She led a round of applause and then, since the ushers continued to stand there at the doors, looking warily at each other and at the emcee, she made shooing motions with her hands. "Go on. Scoot. I want to talk to these people in private," and when they still hesitated, "You'll still get paid for the full seminar. Go on." She walked over to the emcee and said something to him, smiling, and it must have reassured him because he nodded to the ushers and then up at the control room, and the ushers went out.

I looked over at Kildy. She was calmly applying lipstick. I looked back at the stage.

"Are you sure—?" I could see the emcee whisper to Ariaura.

"I'm *fine*," she mouthed back at him.

85

The emcee frowned and then stepped off the stage and over to the side door, and the cameraman at the back began taking his videocam off its tripod. "No, no, Ernesto, not you," Ariaura said, "Keep filming."

She waited as the emcee pulled the last door shut behind him and then walked to the front of the stage and stood there completely silent, her arms stiffly at her sides.

Kildy leaned close to me, her lipstick still in her hand. "Are you thinking the prom scene in *Carrie?*"

I nodded, gauging our distance to the emergency exit. There was a distant sound of a door shutting above us—the control room—and Ariaura clasped her hands together. "Alone at last," she said, smiling. "I thought they'd *never* leave."

Laughter.

"And now that they're gone, I have to say this—" She paused dramatically. "Aren't they *gorgeous?*"

Laughter, applause, and several whistles. Ariaura waited till the noise had died down and then asked, "How many of you were at my seminar last Saturday?"

The mood changed instantly. Several hands went up, but tentatively, and two hoop-earringed women looked at each other with the same nervous glance as the ushers had had.

"Or at the one two weeks ago?" Ariaura asked.

Another couple of hands.

"Well, for those of you who weren't at either, let's just say that lately my seminars have been rather...interesting, to put it mildly."

Scattered nervous laughter.

"And those of you familiar with the spirit world know that's what can happen when we try to make contact with energies beyond our earthly plane. The astral plane can be a dangerous place. There are spirits there beyond our control, false spirits who seek to keep us from enlightenment."

False spirits is right, I thought.

"But I fear them not, for my weapon is the Truth." She somehow managed to say it with a capital T.

I looked over at Kildy. She was leaning forward the way she had at that first seminar, intent on Ariaura's words. She was still holding her mirror and lipstick. "What's she up to?" I whispered to Kildy.

She shook her head, still intent on the stage. "It's not her."

"What?"

"She's channeling."

"Chan—?" I said and looked at the stage.

"No spirit, no matter how dark," Ariaura said, "no matter how dishonest, can stand between me and that Higher Truth."

Applause, more enthusiastic.

"Or keep me from bringing that Truth to all of you." She smiled and spread out her arms. "I'm a fraud, a charlatan, a fake," she said cheerfully. "I've never channeled a cosmic spirit in my life. Isus is something I made up back in 1996, when I was running a pyramid scheme in Dayton, Ohio. The feds were closing in on us, and I'd already been up on charges of mail fraud in '94, so I changed my name—my real name's Bonnie Friehl, by the way, but I was using Doreen Manning in Dayton—and stashed the money in a bank in Chickamauga, Virginia, my home town, and then moved to Miami Beach and did fortune-telling while I worked on perfecting Isus's voice."

I fumbled for my notebook and pen. Bonnie Friehl, Cayman Islands, Miami Beach—

"I did fortune-telling, curses mostly—'Pay me and I'll remove the curse I see hanging over you'—till I had my Isus-impersonation ready and then I contacted this guy I knew in Vegas—"

There was an enormous crash from the rear. Ernesto had dropped his shoulder-held video camera and was heading for the door. And this needed to be on film. But I didn't want to miss anything while I tried to figure out how the camera worked.

I glanced over at Kildy, hoping she was taking notes, but she seemed transfixed by what was happening onstage, her forgotten mirror and lipstick still in her hands, her mouth open. I would have to risk missing a few words. I scrambled to my feet.

"Where are you going?" Kildy whispered.

"I've got to get this on tape."

"We are," she said calmly, and nodded imperceptibly at the lipstick and then the mirror, "Audio...and video."

"I love you," I said.

She nodded. "You'd better get those names down, just in case the police confiscate my makeup as evidence," she said.

"His name was Chuck Venture," Ariaura was saying. "He and I had worked together on a chain-letter scheme. His real name's Harold Vogel, but you probably know him by the name he uses out here, Charles Fred."

Jesus. I scribbled the names down: Harold Vogel, Chuck Venture—

"We'd worked a couple of chain-letter scams together," Ariaura said, "so I told him I wanted him to take me to Salem and set me up in the channeling business."

There was a clank and a thud as Ernesto made it to the door and out. It slammed shut behind him.

"Harold always did have a bad habit of writing everything down," Ariaura said chattily. "'You can't blackmail me, Doreen,' he said. 'Wanna bet?' I said. 'It's all in a safety deposit box in Dayton with instructions to open it if anything happens to me.'" She leaned confidingly forward. "It's not, of course. It's in the safe in my bedroom behind the portrait of Isus. The combination's twelve left, six right, fourteen left." She laughed brightly. "So anyway, he taught me all about how you soften the chumps up in the seminars so they'll tell Isus all about their love life in the private audiences, and then send them copies of the videotapes—"

There were several audible gasps behind me and then the beginnings of a murmur, or possibly a growl, but Ariaura paid no attention—

"—and he introduced me to one of the orderlies at New Beginnings Rehab center, and the deep masseuse at the Willowsage Spa for personal details Isus can use to convince them he knows all-sees all—"

The growl was becoming a roar, but it was scarcely audible over the shouts from outside and the banging on the doors, which were apparently locked from the inside.

"—and how to change my voice and expression to make it look like I'm actually channeling a spirit from beyond—"

It sounded as though the emcee and ushers had found a battering ram. The banging had become shuddering thuds.

"—although I don't think learning all that junk about Lemuria and stuff was necessary," Ariaura said. "I mean, it's obvious you people will believe anything." She smiled beatifically at the audience, as if expecting applause, but the only sound (beside the thuds) was of cell phone keys being hit and women shouting into them. When I glanced around, everybody except Kildy had a phone clapped to their ear.

"Are there any questions?" Ariaura asked brightly.

"Yes," I said. "Are you saying you're the one doing the voice of Isus?"

She smiled pleasedly down at me. "Of course. There's no such thing as channeling spirits from the Great Beyond. Other questions?" She looked past me to the other wildly waving hands. "Yes? The woman in blue?"

"How could you lie to us, you—"

I stepped adroitly in front of her. "Are you saying Todd Phoenix is a fake, too?"

"Oh, yes," Ariaura said. "They're all fakes—Todd Phoenix, Joye Wilde, Randall Mars. Next question? Yes, Miss Ross?"

Kildy stepped forward, still holding the compact and lipstick. "When was the first time you met me?" she asked.

"You don't have to do this," I said.

"Just for the record," she said, flashing me her radiant smile and then turning back to the stage. "Ariaura, had you ever met me before last week?"

"No," she said. "I saw you at Ari—at my seminar, but I didn't meet you till afterwards at the office of the *Jaundiced Eye,* a fine magazine, by the way. I suggest you all take out subscriptions."

"And I'm not your shill?" Kildy persisted.

"No, though I do have them," she said. "The woman in green back there in the sixth row is one," she said, pointing at a plump brunette. "Stand up, Lucy."

Lucy was already scuttling to the door, and so were a thin redhead in a rainbow caftan and an impeccably-tailored sixty-year-old in an Armani suit, with a large number of the audience right on their tails.

"Janine's one, too," Ariaura said, pointing at the redhead. "And Doris. They all help gather personal information for Isus to tell them, so it looks like he 'knows all, sees all.'" She laughed delightedly. "Come up onstage and take a bow, girls."

The 'girls' ignored her. Doris, a pack of elderly women on her heels, pushed open the middle door and shouted, "You've got to stop her!"

The emcee and ushers began pushing their way through the door and toward the stage. The audience was even more determined to get out than they were to get in, but I still didn't have much time. "Are all the psychics you named using blackmail like you?" I asked.

"Ariaura!" the emcee shouted, halfway to the stage and caught in the flood of women. "Stop talking. Anything you say can be held against you."

"Oh, hi, Ken," she said. "Ken's in charge of laundering all our money. Take a bow, Ken! And you, too, Derek and Tad and Jared," she said, indicating the ushers. "The boys pump the audience for information and feed it to me over this," she said, holding up her sacred amulet.

She looked back at me. "I forgot what you asked."

"Are all the pyschics you named using blackmail like you?"

"No, not all of them. Swami Vishnu Jammi uses post-hypnotic suggestion, and Nadrilene's always used extortion."

"What about Charles Fred? What's his scam?"

"Invest—" Ariaura's pin-on mike went suddenly dead. I looked back at the melee. One of the ushers was proudly holding up an unplugged cord.

"Investment fraud," Ariaura shouted, her hands cupped around her mouth. "Chuck tells his marks their dead relations want them to invest in certain stocks. I'd suggest you—"

One of the ushers reached the stage. He grabbed Ariaura by one arm and tried to grab the other.

"—suggest you check out Metra—," Ariaura shouted, flailing at him. "Metracon, Spirilink—"

A second usher appeared, and the two of them managed to pinion her arms. "Crystalcom, Inc—," she said, kicking out at them, "—and Universis. Find out—" She aimed a kick at the groin of one of the ushers that made me flinch. "Get your paws off me."

The emcee stepped in front of her. "That concludes Ariaura's presentation," he said, avoiding her kicking feet. "Thank you all for coming. Videos of—" he said and then thought better of it, "—personally autographed copies of Ariaura's book, *Believe and—*"

"Find out who the majority stockholder is," Ariaura shrieked, struggling. "And ask Chuck what he knows about a check forgery scam Zolita's running in Reno."

"—*It Will Happen* are on sale in the..." the emcee said and gave up. He grabbed for Ariaura's feet. The three of them wrestled her toward the wings.

"One last question!" I shouted, but it was too late. They already had her off the stage. "Why was the baby in the icebox?"

—10—

"...this is the last time you'll see me..."
— H.L. MENCKEN —

◆ ◆ ◆

"It still doesn't prove it was Mencken," I told Kildy. "The whole thing could been a manifestation of Ariaura's—excuse me, Bonnie Friehl's—subconscious, produced by her guilt."

"*Or,*" Kildy said, "there could have been a scam just like the one you postulated, only one of the swindlers fell in love with you and decided she couldn't go through with it."

"Nope, that won't work," I said. "She might have been able to talk Ariaura into calling off the scam, but not into confessing all those crimes."

"If she really committed them," Kildy said. "We don't have any independently verifiable evidence that she is Bonnie Friehl yet." But the fingerprints on her Ohio driver's license matched, and every single lead she'd given us checked out.

We spent the next two months following up on all of them and putting together a massive special issue on "The Great Channeling Swindle." It looked like we were going to have to testify at Ariaura's preliminary hearing, which could have proved awkward, but she and her lawyers got in a big fight over whether or not to use an insanity defense since she was claiming she'd been possessed by the Spirit of Evil and Darkness, and she ended up firing them and turning state's evidence against Charles Fred, Joye Wilde, and several other psychics she hadn't gotten around to mentioning, and it began to look like the magazine might fold because there weren't any scams left to write about.

Fat chance. Within weeks, new mediums and psychics, advertising themselves as "Restorers of Cosmic Ethics" and "the spirit entity you can trust," moved in to fill the void, and a new weight-loss-through-meditation program began packing them in, promising Low-Carb Essence, and Kildy and I were back in business.

"He didn't make any difference at all," Kildy said disgustedly after a standing-room-only seminar on psychic Botox treatments.

"Yeah, he did," I said. "Charles Fred's up on insider trading charges, attendance is down at the Temple of Cosmic Exploration,, and half of L.A.'s psychics are on the lam. And it'll take everybody awhile to come up with new methods for separating people from their money."

"I thought you said it wasn't Mencken."

"I said it didn't *prove* it was Mencken. Rule Number One: Extraordinary claims require extraordinary evidence."

"And you don't think what happened on that stage was extraordinary?"

I had to admit it was. "But it could have been Ariaura herself. She didn't say anything she couldn't have known."

"What about her telling us the combination of her safe? And ordering everybody to subscribe to *The Jaundiced Eye?*"

"It still doesn't prove it was Mencken. It could have been some sort of Bridey-Murphy phenomenon. Ariaura could have had a babysitter who read the *Baltimore Sun* out loud to her when she was a toddler."

Kildy laughed. "You don't believe that."

"I don't believe anything without proof," I said. "I'm a skeptic, remember? And there's nothing that happened on that stage that couldn't be explained rationally."

"Exactly," Kildy said.

"What do you mean, exactly?"

"By their fruits shall ye know them."

"What?"

"I mean it has to have been Mencken because he did exactly what we asked him to do: prove it wasn't a scam and he wasn't a fake and Ariaura was. And do it without proving he was Mencken because if he did, then that proved she was on the level. Which *proves* it was Mencken."

There was no good answer to that kind of crazy illogic except to change the subject, which I did. I kissed her.

And then sent the transcripts of Ariaura's outbursts to UCLA to have the language patterns compared to Mencken's writing. Independently verifiable evidence. And got the taped *The Baby in the Icebox* out of its hiding place down behind the bookcase while Kildy was out of the office, took it home, wrapped it in tin foil, stuck it inside an empty Lean Cuisine box, and hid it—where else?—in the icebox. Old habits die hard.

UCLA sent the transcripts back, saying it wasn't a big enough sample for a conclusive result. So did CalTech. And Duke. So that was that. Which was too bad. It would have been nice to have Mencken back in the fray, even for a little while. He had definitely left too soon.

So Kildy and I would have to pick up where he left off, which meant not only putting "The sons of bitches are gaining on us," on the masthead of *The Jaundiced Eye,* but trying to channel his spirit into every page.

And that didn't just mean exposing shysters and con men. Mencken hadn't been the important force he was because of his rants against creationism and faith-healers and patent medicine, but because of what he'd stood for: the Truth. That's why he'd hated ignorance and superstition and dishonesty so much, because he loved science and reason and logic, and he'd communicated that love, that passion, to his readers with every word he wrote.

That was what we had to do with *The Jaundiced Eye*. It wasn't enough just to expose Ariaura and Swami Vishnu and psychic dentists and meditation Atkins diets. We also had to make our readers as passionate about science and reason as they were about Romtha and luminescence readings. We had to not only tell the truth, but make our readers *want* to believe it.

So, as I say, we were pretty busy for the next few months, revamping the magazine, cooperating with the police, and following up on all the leads Ariaura had given us. We went to Vegas to research the chain-letter scam she and Chuck Venture/Charles Fred had run, after which I came home to put the magazine to bed, and Kildy went to Dayton and then to Chickamauga to follow up on Ariaura's criminal history.

She called last night. "It's me, Rob," she said, sounding excited. "I'm in Chattanooga."

"Chattanooga, *Tennessee?*" I said. "What are you doing there?"

"The prosecutor working on the pyramid scheme case is on a trip to Roanoke, so I can't see him till Monday, and the school board in Zion—that's a little town near here—is trying to pass a law requiring intelligent design to be taught in the public schools. This Zion thing's part of a nationwide program that's going to introduce intelligent design state by state. So, anyway, since I couldn't see the prosecutor, I thought I'd drive over—it's only about fifty miles from Chickamauga—and interview some of the science teachers for that piece on 'The Scopes Trial Eighty Years Out' you were talking about doing."

"And?" I said warily.

"*And,* according to the chemistry teacher, something peculiar happened at the school board meeting. It might be nothing, but I thought I'd better call so you could be looking up flights to Chattanooga, just in case."

Just in case.

"One of the school board members, a Mr.—" she paused as if consulting her notes, "Horace Didlong, was talking about the lack of scientific proof for Darwin's theory, when he suddenly started ranting at the crowd."

"Did the chemistry teacher say what he said?" I asked, hoping I didn't already know.

"She couldn't remember all of it," Kildy said, "but the basketball coach said some of the students had said they intended to tape the meeting and send it to the ACLU, and he'd try to find out if they did and get me a copy. He said it was 'a very odd outburst, almost like he was possessed.'"

"Or drunk," I said. "And neither of them remembers what he said?"

"No, they both do, just not everything. Didlong apparently went on for several minutes. He said he couldn't believe there were still addlepated ignoramuses around who didn't believe in evolution, and what the hell had they been teaching in the schools all this time. The chemistry teacher said the rant went on like that for about five minutes and then broke off, right in the middle of a word, and Didlong went back to talking about how Newton's Second Law makes evolution physically impossible."

"Have you interviewed Didlong?"

"No. I'm going over there as soon as we finish talking, but the chemistry teacher said she heard Didlong's wife ask him what happened, and he looked like he didn't have any idea."

"That doesn't prove it's Mencken," I said.

"I know," she said, "but it *is* Tennessee, and it *is* evolution. And it would be nice if it was him, wouldn't it?"

Nice. H.L. Mencken loose in the middle of Tennessee in the middle of a creationism debate.

"Yeah," I said and grinned, "it would, but it's much more likely Horace Didlong has been smoking something he grew in his backyard. Or is trying to stir up some publicity, à la Judge Roy Moore and his Ten Commandments monument. Do they remember anything else he said?"

"Yes, um…where is it?" she said. "Oh, here it is. He called the other board members a gang of benighted rubes…and then he said he'd take a monkey any day over a school board whose cerebellums were all paralyzed from listening to too much theological bombast…and right at the end, before he broke off, the chemistry teacher said he said, 'I never saw much resemblance to Alice myself.'"

"Alice?" I said. "They're sure he said Alice and not August?"

"Yes, because the chemistry teacher's name is Alice, and she thought he was talking to her, and the chairman of the school-board did, too, because he looked at her and said, 'Alice? What the heck does Alice have to do with intelligent design?' and Didlong said, 'Jamie sure could write, though, even if the bastard did steal my girl. You better be careful I don't steal yours.' Do you know what that means, Rob?"

"Yes," I said. "How long does it take to get a marriage license in Tennessee?"

"I'll find out," Kildy said, sounding pleased, "and then the chairman said, 'You cannot use language like that,' and, according to the chemistry teacher, Didlong said…wait a minute, I need to read it to you so I get it right—it really didn't make any sense—

he said, 'You'd be surprised at what I can do. Like stir up the animals. Speaking of which, that's why the baby was stashed in the icebox. Its mother stuck it inside to keep the tiger from eating it.'"

"I'll be right there," I said.